"THERE WAS NO ONE SO EFFECTIVE AS THE AUSTRIAN
OFFICERS"

THEIR
SILVER WEDDING
JOURNEY

By

W. D. HOWELLS

AUTHOR OF "A HAZARD OF NEW FORTUNES"
"THE LANDLORD AT LION'S HEAD" ETC.

ILLUSTRATED

IN TWO VOLUMES

Vol. I.

NEW YORK AND LONDON
HARPER & BROTHERS PUBLISHERS
MDCCCXCIX

ILLUSTRATIONS

FULL-PAGE

iii

HEAD-PIECES

iv

THEIR SILVER WEDDING JOURNEY

I

"YOU need the rest," said the Business End; "and your wife wants you to go, as well as your doctor. Besides, it's your Sabbatical year, and you could send back a lot of stuff for the magazine."

"Is that your notion of a Sabbatical year?" asked the editor.

"No; I throw that out as a bait to your conscience. You needn't write a line while you're gone. I wish you wouldn't, for your own sake; although every number that hasn't got you in it is a back number for me."

"That's very nice of you, Fulkerson," said the editor. "I suppose you realize that it's *nine* years since we took *Every Other Week* from Dryfoos?"

"Well, that makes it all the more Sabbatical," said Fulkerson. "The two extra years that you've put in here, over and above the old style Sabbatical seven, are just so much more to your credit. It was your right to go, two years ago, and now it's your duty. Couldn't you look at it in that light?"

"I dare say Mrs. March could," the editor assented. "I don't believe she could be brought to regard it as a pleasure on any other terms."

"Of course not," said Fulkerson. "If you won't take a year, take three months, and call it a Sabbatical summer; but go, anyway. You can make up half a dozen numbers ahead, and Tom, here, knows your ways so well that you needn't think about *Every Other Week* from the time you start till the time you try to bribe the customs inspector when you get back. I can take a hack at the editing myself, if Tom's inspiration gives out, and put a little of my advertising fire into the thing." He laid his hand on the shoulder of the young fellow who stood smiling by, and pushed and shook him in the liking there was between them. "Now you *go*, March! Mrs. Fulkerson feels just as I do about it; we had our outing last year, and we want Mrs. March and you to have yours. You let me go down and engage your passage, and—"

"No, no!" the editor rebelled. "I'll think about it;" but as he turned to the work that he was so fond of and so weary of, he tried not

2

to think of the question again, till he closed his desk in the afternoon, and started to walk home; the doctor had said he ought to walk, and he did so, though he longed to ride, and looked wistfully at the passing cars.

He knew he was in a rut, as his wife often said; but if it was a rut, it was a support too; it kept him from wobbling. She always talked as if the flowery fields of youth lay on either side of the dusty road he had been going so long, and he had but to step aside from it, to be among the butterflies and buttercups again; he sometimes indulged this illusion, himself, in a certain ironical spirit which mocked while it caressed the notion. They had a tacit agreement that their youth, if they were ever to find it again, was to be looked for in Europe, where they met when they were young, and they had never been quite without the hope of going back there, some day, for a long sojourn. They had not seen the time when they could do so; they were dreamers, but, as they recognized, even dreaming is not free from care; and in his dream March had been obliged to work pretty steadily, if not too intensely. He had been forced to forego the distinctly literary ambition with which he had started in life because he had their common living to make, and he could not make it by writing graceful verse, or even graceful prose. He had been many years in a sufficiently distasteful business, and he had lost any thought of leaving it when it left him, perhaps because his hold on it had always been rather lax, and he had not been able to conceal that he disliked it. At any rate, he was supplanted in his insurance agency at Boston by a subordinate in his office, and though he was at the same time offered a place of nominal credit in the employ of the company, he was able to decline it in grace of a chance which united the charm of congenial work with the solid advantage of a better salary than he had been getting for work he hated. It was an incredible chance, but it was rendered appreciably real by the necessity it involved that they should leave Boston, where they had lived all their married life, where Mrs. March as well as their children was born, and where all their tender and familiar ties were, and come to New York, where the literary enterprise which formed his chance was to be founded.

It was then a magazine of a new sort, which his business partner had imagined in such leisure as the management of a newspaper syndicate afforded him, and had always thought of getting March to edit. The magazine which is also a book has since been realized elsewhere on more or less prosperous terms, but not for any long period, and *Every Other Week* was apparently the only periodical of the kind conditioned for survival. It was at first backed

4

by unlimited capital, and it had the instant favor of a popular mood, which has since changed, but which did not change so soon that the magazine had not time to establish itself in a wide acceptance. It was now no longer a novelty, it was no longer in the maiden blush of its first success, but it had entered upon its second youth with the reasonable hope of many years of prosperity before it. In fact, it was a very comfortable living for all concerned, and the Marches had the conditions, almost dismayingly perfect, in which they had often promised themselves to go and be young again in Europe, when they rebelled at finding themselves elderly in America. Their daughter was married, and so very much to her mother's mind that she did not worry about her even though she lived so far away as Chicago, still a wild frontier town to her Boston imagination ; and their son as soon as he left college had taken hold on *Every Other Week*, under his father's instruction, with a zeal and intelligence which won him Fulkerson's praise as a chip of the old block. These two liked each other, and worked into each other's hands as cordially and aptly as Fulkerson and March had ever done. It amused the father to see his son offering Fulkerson the same deference which the Business End paid to seniority in March himself ; but, in fact, Fulkerson's forehead was getting, as he said, more intel-

5

lectual every day; and the years were pushing
them all along together.

Still, March had kept on in the old rut, and
one day he fell down in it. He had a long
sickness, and when he was well of it, he was
so slow in getting his grip of work again that
he was sometimes deeply discouraged. His
wife shared his depression, whether he showed
or whether he hid it, and when the doctor advised his going abroad, she abetted the doctor
with all the strength of a woman's hygienic
intuitions. March himself willingly consented,
at first; but as soon as he got strength for his
work, he began to temporize and to demur.
He said that he believed it would do him just
as much good to go to Saratoga, where they
always had such a good time, as to go to Carlsbad; and Mrs. March had been obliged several
times to leave him to his own undoing; she
always took him more vigorously in hand afterwards.

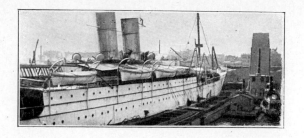

II

WHEN he got home from the *Every Other Week* office, the afternoon of that talk with the Business End, he wanted to laugh with his wife at Fulkerson's notion of a Sabbatical year. She did not think it was so very droll; she even urged it seriously against him, as if she had now the authority of Holy Writ for forcing him abroad; she found no relish of absurdity in the idea that it was his duty to take this rest which had been his right before.

He abandoned himself to a fancy which had been working to the surface of his thought. "We could call it our Silver Wedding Journey, and go round to all the old places, and see them in the reflected light of the past."

"Oh, we *could!*" she responded passionately; and he had now the delicate responsibility of persuading her that he was joking.

7

He could think of nothing better than a return to Fulkerson's absurdity. "It would be our Silver Wedding Journey just as it would be my Sabbatical year—a good deal after date. But I suppose that would make it all the more silvery."

She faltered in her elation. "Didn't you *say* a Sabbatical year yourself?" she demanded.

"Fulkerson said it; but it was a figurative expression."

"And I suppose the Silver Wedding Journey was a figurative expression too!"

"It was a notion that tempted me; I thought you would enjoy it. Don't you suppose I should be glad too, if we could go over, and find ourselves just as we were when we first met there?"

"No; I don't believe now that you care anything about it."

"Well, it couldn't be done, anyway; so that doesn't matter."

"It *could* be done, if you were a mind to think so. And it would be the greatest inspiration to you. You are always longing for some chance to do original work, to get away from your editing, but you've let the time slip by without really trying to do anything; I don't call those little studies of yours in the magazine anything; and now you won't take the chance that's almost forcing itself upon you. You could write an original book of the nicest

"'WE COULD CALL IT OUR SILVER WEDDING JOURNEY'"

kind; mix up travel and fiction; get some love in."

"Oh, that's the stalest kind of thing!"

"Well, but you could see it from a perfectly new point of view. You could look at it as a sort of dispassionate witness, and treat it humorously — of course it *is* ridiculous — and do something entirely fresh."

"It wouldn't work. It would be carrying water on both shoulders. The fiction would kill the travel, the travel would kill the fiction; the love and the humor wouldn't mingle any more than oil and vinegar."

"Well, and what is better than a salad?"

"But this would be all salad-dressing, and nothing to put it on." She was silent, and he yielded to another fancy. "We might imagine coming upon our former selves over there, and travelling round with them—a wedding journey *en partie carrée.*"

"Something like that. I call it a very poetical idea," she said with a sort of provisionality, as if distrusting another ambush.

"It isn't so bad," he admitted. "How young we were, in those days!"

"Too young to know what a good time we were having," she said, relaxing her doubt for the retrospect. "I don't feel as if I really saw Europe, then; I was too inexperienced, too ignorant, too simple. I should like to go, just to make sure that I had been." He was smiling again in the way he had when anything occurred to him that amused him, and she demanded, "What is it?"

"Nothing. I was wishing we could go in the consciousness of people who actually hadn't been before—carry them all through Europe and let them see it in the old, simple-hearted American way."

She shook her head. "You couldn't! They've all been!"

"All but about sixty or seventy millions," said March.

"Well, those are just the millions you don't know, and couldn't imagine."

"I'm not so sure of that."

"And even if you could imagine them, you couldn't make them interesting. All the interesting ones have been, anyway."

"Some of the uninteresting ones too. I used to meet some of that sort over there. I believe I would rather chance it for my pleasure with those that hadn't been."

"Then why not do it? I know you could get something out of it."

"It might be a good thing," he mused, "to take a couple who had passed their whole life here in New York, too poor and too busy ever to go, and had a perfect famine for Europe all the time. I could have them spend their Sunday afternoons going aboard the different boats, and looking up their accommodations. I could have them sail, in imagination, and discover an imaginary Europe, and give their grotesque misconceptions of it from travels and novels against a background of purely American experience. We needn't go abroad to manage that. I think it would be rather nice."

"I don't think it would be nice in the least," said Mrs. March, "and if you don't want to talk seriously, I would rather not talk at all."

"Well, then, let us talk about our Silver Wedding Journey."

"I see. You merely want to tease, and I am not in the humor for it."

She said this in a great many different ways, and then she was really silent. He perceived that she was hurt; and he tried to win her back to good-humor. He asked her if she would not like to go over to Hoboken and look at one of the Hanseatic League steamers, some day ; and she refused. When he sent the next day and got a permit to see the boat, she consented to go.

III

HE was one of those men who live from the inside outward; he often took a hint for his actions from his fancies; and now because he had fancied some people going to look at steamers on Sundays, he chose the next Sunday himself for their visit to the Hanseatic boat at Hoboken. To be sure it was a leisure day with him, but he might have taken the afternoon of any other day, for that matter, and it was really that invisible thread of association which drew him.

The *Colmannia* had been in long enough to have made her toilet for the outward voyage, and was looking her best. She was tipped and edged with shining brass, without and within, and was red-carpeted and white-painted as only a ship knows how to be. A little uniformed steward ran before the visitors, and showed them through the dim white corridors into

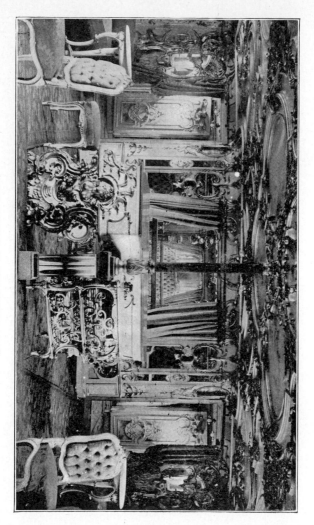

"THE LUXURY OF THE MUSIC-ROOM"

typical state - rooms on the different decks ; and then let them verify their first impression of the grandeur of the dining-saloon, and the luxury of the ladies' parlor and music-room. March made his wife observe that the tables and sofas and easy-chairs, which seemed so carelessly scattered about, were all suggestively screwed fast to the floor against rough weather ; and he amused himself with the heavy German browns and greens and coppers of the decorations, which he said must have been studied in color from sausage, beer, and spinach, to the effect of those large march-panes in the roof. She laughed with him at the tastelessness of the race which they were destined to marvel at more and more ; but she made him own that the stewardesses whom they saw were charmingly like serving - maids in the *Fliegende Blätter ;* when they went ashore she challenged his silence for some assent to her own conclusion that the *Colmannia* was perfect.

"She has only one fault," he assented. "She's a ship."

"Yes," said his wife, " and I shall want to look at the *Norumbia* before I decide."

Then he saw that it was only a question which steamer they should take, and not whether they should take any. He explained, at first gently and afterwards savagely, that their visit to the *Colmannia* was quite enough for him, and that the vessel was not built that he would be willing to cross the Atlantic in.

When a man has gone so far as that he has committed himself to the opposite course in almost so many words ; and March was neither surprised nor abashed when he discovered himself, before they reached home, offering his wife many reasons why they should go to Europe. She answered to all, No, he had made her realize the horror of it so much that she was glad to give it up. She gave it up, with the best feeling ; all that she would ask of him was that he should never mention Europe to her again. She could imagine how much he disliked to go, if such a ship as the *Colmannia* did not make him want to go.

At the bottom of his heart he knew that he had not used her very well. He had kindled her fancy with those notions of a Sabbatical year and a Silver Wedding Journey, and when she was willing to renounce both he had persisted in taking her to see the ship, only to tell her afterwards that he would not go abroad on any account. It was by a psychological juggle which some men will understand that he allowed himself the next day to get the sailings of the *Norumbia* from the steamship office ; he also got a plan of the ship showing the most available state-rooms, so that they might be able to choose between her and the *Colmannia* from all the facts.

18

IV

F ROM this time their decision to go was
none the less explicit because so perfectly
tacit.

They began to amass maps and guides. She
got a Baedeker for Austria and he got a Brad-
shaw for the continent, which was never of the
least use there, but was for the present a mine
of unavailable information. He got a phrase-
book, too, and tried to rub up his German.
He used to read German, when he was a boy,
with a young enthusiasm for its romantic
poetry, and now, for the sake of Schiller and
Uhland and Heine, he held imaginary con-
versations with a barber, a bootmaker, and
a banker, and tried to taste the joy which he
had not known in the language of those poets
for a whole generation. He perceived, of course,
that unless the barber, the bootmaker, and
the banker answered him in terms which the

author of the phrase-book directed them to use, he should not get on with them beyond his first question ; but he did not allow this to spoil his pleasure in it. In fact, it was with a tender emotion that he realized how little the world, which had changed in everything else so greatly, had changed in its ideal of a phrase-book.

Mrs. March postponed the study of her Baedeker to the time and place for it, and addressed herself to the immediate business of ascertaining the respective merits of the *Colmannia* and *Norumbia*. She carried on her researches solely among persons of her own sex ; its experiences were alone of that positive character which brings conviction, and she valued them equally at first or second hand. She heard of ladies who would not cross in any boat but the *Colmannia*, and who waited for months to get a room on her ; she talked with ladies who said that nothing would induce them to cross in her. There were ladies who said she had twice the motion that the *Norumbia* had, and the vibration from her twin screws was frightful ; it always was, on those twin-screw boats, and it did not affect their testimony with Mrs. March that the *Norumbia* was a twin-screw boat too. It was repeated to her in the third or fourth degree of hearsay that the discipline on the *Colmannia* was as perfect as on the Cunarders ; ladies whose friends had tried every line assured her that the table of the *Norumbia* was almost as good as the table of the French boats. To the best of the belief of lady witnesses still living who had friends on board, the *Colmannia* had once got aground, and the *Norumbia* had once had her bridge carried off by a tidal wave ; or it might be the *Colmannia ;* they promised to ask and let her know. Their lightest word availed with her against the most solemn assurances of their husbands, fathers, or brothers, who might be all very well on land, but in navigation were not to be trusted ; they would say anything from a reckless and culpable optimism. She obliged March all the same to ask among them, but she recognized their guilty insincerity when he came home saying that one man had told him you could have played croquet on the deck of the *Colmannia* the whole way over when he crossed, and another that he never saw the racks on in three passages he had made in the *Norumbia*.

The weight of evidence was, he thought, in favor of the *Norumbia*, but when they went another Sunday to Hoboken, and saw the ship, Mrs. March liked her so much less than the *Colmannia* that she could hardly wait for Monday to come ; she felt sure all the good rooms on the *Colmannia* would be gone before they could engage one.

From a consensus of the nerves of all the ladies left in town so late in the season, she knew that the only place on any steamer where your room ought to be was probably just where they could not get it. If you went too high, you felt the rolling terribly, and people tramping up and down on the promenade under your window kept you awake the whole night; if you went too low, you felt the engine thump, thump, thump in your head the whole way over. If you went too far forward, you got the pitching; if you went aft, on the kitchen side, you got the smell of the cooking. The only place, really, was just back of the dining-saloon on the south side of the ship; it was smooth there, and it was quiet, and you had the sun in your window all the way over. He asked her if he must take their room there or nowhere, and she answered that he must do his best, but that she would not be satisfied with any other place.

In his despair he went down to the steamer office, and took a room which one of the clerks said was the best. When he got home, it appeared from reference to the ship's plan that it was the very room his wife had wanted from the beginning, and she praised him as if he had used a wisdom beyond his sex in getting it.

He was in the enjoyment of his unmerited honor when a belated lady came with her husband for an evening call, before going into the country. At sight of the plans of steamers on the Marches' table, she expressed the greatest wonder and delight that they were going to

Europe. They had supposed everybody knew it, by this time, but she said she had not heard a word of it; and she went on with some felicitations which March found rather unduly filial. In getting a little past the prime of life he did not like to be used with too great consideration of his years, and he did not think that he and his wife were so old that they need be treated as if they were going on a golden wedding journey, and heaped with all sorts of impertinent prophecies of their enjoying it *so* much and being *so* much the better for the little outing! Under his breath, he confounded this lady for her impudence; but he schooled himself to let her rejoice at their going on a Hanseatic boat, because the Germans were always so *careful* of you. She made her husband agree with her, and it came out that he had crossed several times on both the *Colmannia* and the *Norumbia*. He volunteered to say that the *Colmannia* was a capital sea-boat; she did not have her nose under water all the time; she was steady as a rock; and the captain and the kitchen were simply out of sight; some people did call her unlucky.

"Unlucky?" Mrs. March echoed, faintly. "Why do they call her unlucky?"

"Oh, I don't know. People will say anything about any boat. You know she broke her shaft, once, and once she got caught in the ice."

Mrs. March joined him in deriding the superstition of people, and she parted gayly with this over-good young couple. As soon as they were gone, March knew that she would say : "You must change that ticket, my dear. We will go in the *Norumbia*."

"Suppose I can't get as good a room on the *Norumbia* ?"

"Then we must stay."

In the morning after a night so bad that it was worse than no night at all, she said she would go to the steamship's office with him and question them up about the *Colmannia*. The people there had never heard she was called an unlucky boat ; they knew of nothing disastrous in her history. They were so frank and so full in their denials, and so kindly patient of Mrs. March's anxieties, that he saw every word was carrying conviction of their insincerity to her. At the end she asked what rooms were left on the *Norumbia*, and the clerk whom they had fallen to looked through his passenger list with a shaking head. He was afraid there was nothing they would like.

"But we would take *anything*," she entreated, and March smiled to think of his innocence in supposing for a moment that she had ever dreamed of not going.

"We merely want the best," he put in. "One flight up, no noise or dust, with sun in all the windows, and a place for fire on rainy days."

24

They must be used to a good deal of American joking which they do not understand, in the foreign steamship offices. The clerk turned unsmilingly to one of his superiors and asked him some question in German which March could not catch, perhaps because it formed no part of a conversation with a barber, a bootmaker, or a banker. A brief drama followed, and then the clerk pointed to a room on the plan of the *Norumbia* and said it had just been given up, and they could have it if they would decide to take it at once.

They looked, and it was in the very place of their room on the *Colmannia;* it was within one of being the same number. It was so providential, if it was providential at all, that they were both humbly silent a moment ; even Mrs. March was silent. In this supreme moment she would not prompt her husband by a word, a glance, and it was from his own free will that he said, " We will take it."

He thought it was his free will, but perhaps one's will is never free ; and this may have been an instance of pure determinism from all the events before it. No event that followed affected it, though the day after they had taken their passage on the *Norumbia* he heard that she had once been in the worst sort of storm in the month of August. He felt obliged to impart the fact to his wife, but she said that it proved nothing for or against the ship, and confounded him more by her reason than by all her previous unreason. Reason is what a man is never prepared for in women ; perhaps because he finds it so seldom in men.

V

DURING nearly the whole month that now passed before the date of sailing it seemed to March that in some familiar aspects New York had never been so interesting. He had not easily reconciled himself to the place after his many years of Boston; but he had got used to the ugly grandeur, to the noise and the rush, and he had divined more and more the careless good-nature and friendly indifference of the vast, sprawling, ungainly metropolis. There were happy moments when he felt a poetry unintentional and unconscious in it, and he thought there was no point more favorable for the sense of this than Stuyvesant Square, where they had a flat. Their windows looked down into its tree-tops, and across them to the truncated towers of St. George's, and to the plain red-brick, white-trimmed front of the Friends' Meeting-House;

and at all hours of the day he liked going into it. He came and went between his dwelling and his office through the two places that form the square, and after dinner his wife and he had a habit of finding seats by one of the fountains in Livingston Place, among the fathers and mothers of the hybrid East Side children swarming there at play. The elders read their English or Italian or German or Yiddish journals, or gossiped, or merely sat still and stared away the day's fatigue ; while the little ones raced in and out among them, crying and laughing, quarrelling and kissing. Sometimes a mother darted forward and caught her child from the brink of the basin ; another taught hers to walk, holding it tightly up behind by its short skirts ; another publicly bared her breast and nursed her baby to sleep.

While they still dreamed, but never thought, of going to Europe, the Marches often said how European all this was ; if these women had brought their knitting or sewing it would have been quite European ; but as soon as they had decided to go, it all began to seem poignantly American. In like manner, before the conditions of their exile changed, and they still pined for the Old World, they contrived a very agreeable illusion of it by dining now and then at an Austrian restaurant in Union Square ; but later, when they began to be homesick for the American scenes they had not yet left, they had a keener retrospective joy in the strictly New York sunset they were bowed out into.

The sunsets were uncommonly characteristic that May in Union Square. They were the color of the red stripes in the American flag, and when they were seen through the delirious architecture of the Broadway side, or down the perspective of the cross-streets, where the elevated trains silhouetted themselves against their pink, they imparted a feeling of pervasive Americanism in which all impression of alien savors and civilities was lost. One evening a fire flamed up in Hoboken, and burned for hours against the west, in the lurid crimson tones of a conflagration as memorably and appealingly native as the colors of the sunset.

The weather for nearly the whole month was of a mood familiar enough in our early summer, and it was this which gave the sunsets their vitreous pink. A thrilling coolness followed a first blaze of heat, and in the long respite the thoughts almost went back to winter flannels. But at last a hot wave was telegraphed from the West, and the week before the *Norumbia* sailed was an anguish of burning days and breathless nights, which fused all regrets and reluctances in the hope of escape, and made the exiles of two continents long for the sea with no care for either shore.

VI

THEIR steamer was to sail early; they
were up at dawn because they had scarcely lain down, and March crept out into
the square for a last breath of its morning air
before breakfast. He was now eager to be gone;
he had broken with habit, and he wished to put
all traces of the past out of sight. But this was
curiously like all other early mornings in his
consciousness, and he could not alienate himself from the wonted environment. He stood
talking on every-day terms of idle speculation
with the familiar policeman, about a stray par-
rot in the top of one of the trees, where it
screamed and clawed at the dead branch to
which it clung. Then he went carelessly in-
doors again as if he were secure of reading the
reporter's story of it in that next day's paper
which he should not see.

The sense of an inseverable continuity persisted through the breakfast, which was like other breakfasts in the place they would be leaving in summer shrouds just as they always left it at the end of June. The illusion was even heightened by the fact that their son was to be in the apartment all summer, and it would not be so much shut up as usual. The heavy trunks had been sent to the ship by express the afternoon before, and they had only themselves and their state-room baggage to transport to Hoboken; they came down to a carriage sent from a neighboring livery-stable, and exchanged good-mornings with a driver they knew by name.

March had often fancied it a chief advantage of living in New York that you could drive to the steamer and start for Europe as if you were starting for Albany; he was in the enjoyment of this advantage now, but somehow it was not the consolation he had expected. He knew, of course, that if they had been coming from Boston, for instance, to sail in the *Norumbia*, they would probably have gone on board the night before, and sweltered through its heat among the strange smells and noises of the dock and wharf, instead of breakfasting at their own table, and smoothly bowling down the asphalt on to the ferry-boat, and so to the very foot of the gangway at the ship's side, all in the cool of the early morning. But though he had now the cool of the early morning on these conditions, there was by no means enough of it. The sun was already burning the life out of the air, with the threat of another day of the terrible heat that had prevailed for a week past ; and that last breakfast at home had not been gay, though it had been lively, in a fashion, through Mrs. March's efforts to convince her son that she did not want him to come and see them off. Of her daughter's coming all the way from Chicago there was no question, and she reasoned that if he did not come to say good-bye on board it would be the same as if they were not going.

"Don't you want to go?" March asked with an obscure resentment.

"I don't want to *seem* to go," she said with the calm of those who have logic on their side.

As she drove away with her husband she was not so sure of her satisfaction in the feint she had arranged, though when she saw the ghastly partings of people on board, she was glad she had not allowed her son to come. She kept saying this to herself, and when they climbed to the ship from the wharf, and found themselves in the crowd that choked the saloons and promenades and passages and stairways and landings, she said it more than once to her husband.

She heard weary elders pattering empty politenesses of farewell with friends who had

THE STEAMER LEAVING THE WHARF

come to see them off, as they stood withdrawn
in such refuges as the ship's architecture afforded, or submitted to be pushed and twirled about
by the surging throng when they got in its way.
She pitied these in their affliction, which she
perceived that they could not lighten or shorten,
but she had no patience with the young girls,
who broke into shrieks of nervous laughter at the
coming of certain young men, and kept laughing
and beckoning till they made the young men
see them ; and then stretched their hands to
them and stood screaming and shouting to
them across the intervening heads and shoulders. Some girls, of those whom no one had
come to bid good-bye, made themselves merry,
or at least noisy, by rushing off to the dining-
room and looking at the cards on the bouquets
heaping the tables, to find whether any one had
sent them flowers. Others whom young men
had brought bunches of violets hid their noses in
them, and dropped their fans and handkerchiefs
and card-cases, and thanked the young men for
picking them up. Others had got places in the
music-room, and sat there with open boxes of
long-stemmed roses in their laps, and talked up
into the faces of the men, with becoming lifts
and slants of their eyes and chins. In the midst
of the turmoil children struggled against people's feet and knees, and bewildered mothers
flew at the ship's officers and battered them
with questions alien to their respective func-

tions as they amiably stifled about in their thick uniforms.

Sailors slung over the ship's side on swinging seats were placidly smearing it with paint at that last moment ; the bulwarks were thickly set with the heads and arms of passengers who were making signs to friends on shore, or calling messages to them that lost themselves in louder noises midway. Some of the women in the steerage were crying ; they were probably not going to Europe for pleasure like the first-cabin passengers, or even for their health ; on the wharf below March saw the face of one young girl twisted with weeping, and he wished he had not seen it. He turned from it, and looked into the eyes of his son, who was laughing at his shoulder. He said that he had to come down with a good-bye letter from his sister, which he made an excuse for following them ; but he had always meant to see them off, he owned. The letter had just come with a special delivery stamp, and it warned them that she had sent another good-bye letter with some flowers on board. Mrs. March scolded at them both, but with tears in her eyes, and in the renewed stress of parting which he thought he had put from him, March went on taking note, as with alien senses, of the scene before him, while they all talked on together, and repeated the nothings they had said already.

A rank odor of beet-root sugar rose from the

far-branching sheds where some freight steamers of the line lay, and seemed to mingle chemically with the noise which came up from the wharf next to the *Norumbia*. The mass of spectators deepened and dimmed away into the shadow of the roofs, and along its front came files of carriages and trucks and carts, and discharged the arriving passengers and their baggage, and were lost in the crowd, which they penetrated like slow currents, becoming clogged and arrested from time to time, and then beginning to move again.

The passengers incessantly mounted by the canvas-draped galleries, leading, fore and aft, into the ship. Bare - headed, blue - jacketed, brass-buttoned stewards dodged skilfully in and out among them with their hand-bags, hold-alls, hat-boxes, and state-room trunks, and ran before them into the different depths and heights where they hid these burdens, and then ran back for more. Some of the passengers followed and made sure that their things were put in the right places; but most of them remained wedged among the earlier comers, or pushed aimlessly in and out of the doors of the promenades.

The baggage for the hold continually rose in huge blocks from the wharf, with a loud clucking of the tackle, and sank into the open maw of the ship, momently gathering herself for her long race seaward with harsh hissings and rattlings and gurglings. There was no apparent reason why it should all or any of it end, but there came a moment when there began to be warnings that were almost threats of the end. The ship's whistle sounded, as if marking a certain interval; and Mrs. March humbly entreated, sternly commanded, her son to go ashore, or else be carried to Europe. They disputed whether that was the last signal or not; she was sure it was, and she appealed to March, who was moved against his reason. He affected to talk calmly with his son, and gave him some last charges about *Every Other Week*.

Some people now interrupted their leave-taking; but the arriving passengers only arrived more rapidly at the gangways; the bulks of baggage swung more swiftly into the air. A bell rang, and there rose women's cries, " Oh, that is the shore-bell !" and men's protests, " It is only the first bell !" More and more began to descend the gangways, fore and aft, and soon outnumbered those who were coming aboard.

March tried not to be nervous about his son's lingering; he was ashamed of his anxiety; but he said in a low voice, " Better be off, Tom."

His mother now said she did not care if Tom were really carried to Europe; and at last he said, Well, he guessed he must go ashore, as if there had been no question of that before; and then she clung to him and would not let him go; but she acquired merit with herself at last by pushing him into the gangway with her own hands : he nodded and waved his hat from its foot, and mixed with the crowd.

Presently there was hardly any one coming aboard, and the sailors began to undo the lashings of the gangways from the ship's side; files of men on the wharf laid hold of their rails ; the stewards guarding their approach looked up for the signal to come aboard ; and in vivid pantomime forbade some belated leave-takers to ascend. These stood aside, exchanging bows and grins with the friends whom they could not reach ; they all tried to make one another hear some last words. The moment came when the saloon gangway was detached ; then it was pulled ashore, and the section of the bulwarks opening to it was locked, not to be unlocked on this side of the world. An indefinable impulse communicated itself to the steamer : while it still seemed motionless it moved. The thick spread of faces on the wharf, which had looked at times like some sort of strange flowers in a level field, broke into a universal tremor, and the air above was filled with hats and handkerchiefs, as if with the flight of birds rising from the field.

The Marches tried to make out their son's face ; they believed that they did ; but they decided that they had not seen him, and his mother said that she was glad ; it would only have made it harder to bear, though she was glad he had come over to say good-bye : it had seemed so unnatural that he should not, when everybody else was saying good-bye.

On the wharf color was now taking the place of form ; the scene ceased to have the effect of an instantaneous photograph ; it was like an impressionistic study. As the ship swung free of the shed and got into the stream, the shore lost reality. Up to a certain moment, all was still New York, all was even Hoboken ; then amidst the grotesque and monstrous shows of the architecture on either shore March felt himself at sea and on the way to Europe.

The fact was accented by the trouble people were already making with the deck-steward about their steamer chairs, which they all wanted put in the best places, and March, with a certain heartache, was involuntarily verifying the instant in which he ceased to be of his native shores while still in full sight of them, when he suddenly reverted to them, and as it were landed on them again in an incident that held him breathless. A man, bareheaded, and with his arms flung wildly abroad, came flying down the promenade from the steerage. " Capitan ! Capitan ! There is a *woman !*" he shouted in nondescript English. " She must go hout ! She must go *hout !*" Some vital fact imparted itself to the ship's command and seemed to penetrate to the ship's heart ; she stopped, as if with a sort of majestic relenting. A tug panted

"THEIR STEAMER CHAIRS IN THE BEST PLACES"

to her side, and lifted a ladder to it ; the bareheaded man, and a woman gripping a baby in
her arms, sprawled safely down its rungs to
the deck of the tug, and the steamer moved
seaward again.

"What is it?" Oh, what is it?" his wife demanded of March's share of their common
ignorance. A young fellow passing stopped
as if arrested by the tragic note in her voice,
and explained that the woman had left three
little children locked up in her tenement while
she came to bid some friends on board good-bye.

He passed on, and Mrs. March said, "What
a charming face he had!" even before she
began to wreak upon that wretched mother
the overwrought sympathy which makes good
women desire the punishment of people who
have escaped danger. She would not hear any
excuse for her. "Her children oughtn't to have
been out of her mind for an instant."

"Don't you want to send back a line to ours
by the pilot?" he asked.

She started from him. "Oh, was I really
beginning to *forget* them?"

In the saloon where people were scattered
about writing pilot's letters she made him join
her in an impassioned epistle of farewell, which
once more left none of the nothings unsaid that
they had many times repeated. She would
not let him put the stamp on, for fear it would
not stick, and she had an agonizing moment of

43

doubt whether it ought not to be a German stamp ; she was not pacified till the steward in charge of the mail decided.

"I shouldn't have forgiven myself," March said, "if we hadn't let Tom know that twenty minutes after he left us we were still alive and well."

"It's to Bella, too," she reasoned.

He found her making their state-room look homelike with their familiar things when he came with their daughter's steamer letter and the flowers and fruit she had sent. She said, Very well, they would all keep, and went on with her unpacking. He asked her if she did not think these home things made it rather ghastly, and she said if he kept on in that way she should certainly go back on the pilot-boat. He perceived that her nerves were spent. He had resisted the impulse to an ill-timed joke about the life-preservers under their berths when the sound of the breakfast-horn, wavering first in the distance, found its way nearer and clearer down their corridor.

VII

IN one of the many visits to the steamship
office which his wife's anxieties obliged him
to make, March had discussed the question
of seats in the dining-saloon. At first he had
his ambition for the captain's table, but they
convinced him more easily than he afterwards
convinced Mrs. March that the captain's table
had become a superstition of the past, and conferred no special honor. It proved in the event
that the captain of the *Norumbia* had the good
feeling to dine in a lower saloon among the
passengers who paid least for their rooms.
But while the Marches were still in their ignorance of this, they decided to get what adventure they could out of letting the head
steward put them where he liked, and they
came in to breakfast with a careless curiosity
to see what he had done for them.

There seemed scarcely a vacant place in the

huge saloon ; through the oval openings in the centre they looked down into the lower saloon and up into the music-room, as thickly thronged with breakfasters. The tables were brightened with the bouquets and the floral designs of ships, anchors, harps, and doves sent to the lady passengers, and at one time the Marches thought they were going to be put before a steam-yacht realized to the last detail in blue and white violets. The ports of the saloon were open, and showed the level sea ; the ship rode with no motion except the tremor from her screws. The sound of talking and laughing rose with the clatter of knives and forks and the clash of crockery ; the homely smell of the coffee and steak and fish mixed with the spice of the roses and carnations ; the stewards ran hither and thither, and a young foolish joy of travel welled up in the elderly hearts of the pair. When the head steward turned out the swivel-chairs where they were to sit they both made an inclination towards the people already at table, as if it had been a company at some far forgotten table d'hôte in the later sixties. The head steward seemed to understand as well as speak English, but the table-stewards had only an effect of English, which they eked out with " Bleace !" for all occasions of inquiry, apology, and reassurance, as the equivalent of their native "*Bitte !*" Otherwise there was no reason to suppose that they did not speak Ger-

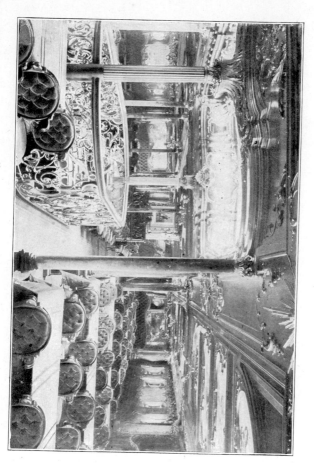

"SEATS IN THE DINING-SALOON"

man, which was the language of a good half of the passengers. The stewards looked English, however, in conformity to what seems the ideal of every kind of foreign seafaring people, and that went a good way towards making them intelligible.

March, to whom his wife mainly left their obeisance, made it so tentative that if it should meet no response he could feel that it had been nothing more than a forward stoop, such as was natural in sitting down. He need not really have taken this precaution; those whose eyes he caught more or less nodded in return. A nice-looking boy of thirteen or fourteen, who had the place on the left of the lady in the sofa seat under the port, bowed with almost magisterial gravity, and made the lady on the sofa smile, as if she were his mother and understood him. March decided that she had been some time a widow; and he easily divined that the young couple on her right had been so little time husband and wife that they would rather not have it known. Next them was a young lady whom he did not at first think so good-looking as she proved later to be, though she had at once a pretty nose, with a slight upward slant at the point, long eyes under fallen lashes, a straight forehead, not too high, and a mouth which perhaps the exigencies of breakfasting did not allow its characteristic expression. She had what Mrs. March thought interesting hair,

of a dull black, roughly rolled away from her
forehead and temples in a fashion not particu-
larly becoming to her, and she had the air of
not looking so well as she might if she had
chosen. The elderly man on her right, it was
easy to see, was her father ; they had a family
likeness, though his fair hair, now ashen with
age, was so different from hers. He wore his
beard cut in the fashion of the Second Empire,
with a Louis Napoleonic mustache, imperial,
and chin tuft ; his neat head was cropped close,
and there was something Gallic in its effect and
something remotely military : he had blue
eyes, really less severe than he meant, though
he frowned a good deal, and managed them
with glances of a staccato quickness, as if
challenging a potential disagreement with his
opinions.

The gentleman on his right, who sat at the
head of the table, was of the humorous, subi-
ronical American expression, and a smile at
the corner of his kindly mouth, under an iron-
gray full beard cut short, at once questioned
and tolerated the new-comers as he glanced at
them. He responded to March's bow almost
as decidedly as the nice boy, whose mother he
confronted at the other end of the table, and
with his comely bulk formed an interesting
contrast to her vivid slightness. She was brill-
iantly dark, behind the gleam of the gold-
rimmed glasses perched on her pretty nose.

If the talk had been general before the Marches came, it did not at once renew itself in that form. Nothing was said while they were having their first struggle with the table-stewards, who repeated the order as if to show how fully they had misunderstood it. The gentleman at the head of the table intervened at last, and then, "I'm obliged to you," March said, "for your German. I left mine in a phrase-book in my other coat pocket."

"Oh, I wasn't speaking German," said the other. "It was merely their kind of English."

The company were in the excitement of a novel situation which disposes people to acquaintance, and this exchange of small pleasantries made every one laugh, except the father and daughter; but they had the effect of being tacitly amused.

The mother of the nice boy said to Mrs. March, "You may not get what you ordered, but it will be good."

"Even if you don't know what it is!" said the young bride, and then blushed, as if she had been too bold.

Mrs. March liked the blush and the young bride for it, and she asked, "Have you ever been on one of these German boats before? They seem very comfortable."

"Oh, dear, no! we've never been on *any* boat before." She made a little petted mouth of deprecation, and added simple - heartedly, "My husband was going out on business, and he thought he might as well take me along."

The husband seemed to feel himself brought in by this, and said he did not see why they should not make it a pleasure-trip, too. They put themselves in a position to be patronized by their deference, and in the pauses of his talk with the gentleman at the head of the table, March heard his wife abusing their inexperience to be unsparingly instructive about European travel. He wondered whether she would be afraid to own that it was nearly thirty years since she had crossed the ocean ; though that might have seemed recent to people who had never crossed at all.

They listened with respect as she boasted in what an anguish of wisdom she had decided between the *Colmannia* and the *Norumbia.* The bride said she did not know there was such a difference in steamers, but when Mrs. March perfervidly assured her that there was all the difference in the world, she submitted and said she supposed she ought to be thankful that they had hit upon the right one. They had telegraphed for berths and taken what was given them ; their room seemed to be very nice.

"Oh," said Mrs. March, and her husband knew that she was saying it to reconcile them to the inevitable, " *all* the rooms on the *Norum-*

bia are nice.   The only difference is that if they are on the south side you have the sun."

"I'm not sure which is the south side," said the bride.   "We seem to have been going west ever since we started, and I feel as if we should reach home in the morning if we had a good night.   Is the ocean always so smooth as this?"

"Oh, *dear*, no!" said Mrs. March.   "It's *never* so smooth as this," and she began to be outrageously authoritative about the ocean weather.   She ended by declaring that the June passages were always good, and that if the ship kept a southerly course they would have no fogs and no icebergs.   She looked round, and caught her husband's eye.   "What is it?   Have I been bragging?   Well, you understand," she added to the bride, "I've only been over once, a great while ago, and I don't really know anything about it," and they laughed together.   "But I talked so much with people after we decided to go, that I feel as if I had been a hundred times."

"I know," said the other lady, with caressing intelligence.   "That is just the way with—" She stopped, and looked at the young man whom the head steward was bringing up to take the vacant place next to March.   He came forward stuffing his cap into the pocket of his blue serge sack, and smiled down on the company with such happiness in his gay eyes that March wondered what chance at this late day could have given any human creature his content so absolute, and what calamity could be lurking round the corner to take it out of him. The new-comer looked at March as if he knew him, and March saw at a second glance that he was the young fellow who had told him about the mother put off after the start. He asked him whether there was any change in the weather yet outside, and he answered eagerly, as if the chance to put his happiness into the mere sound of words were a favor done him, that their ship had just spoken one of the big Hanseatic mail-boats, and she had signalled back that she had met ice; so that they would probably keep a southerly course, and not have it cooler till they were off the Banks.

The mother of the boy said, "I thought we must be off the Banks when I came out of my room, but it was only the electric fan at the foot of the stairs."

"That was what *I* thought," said Mrs. March. "I almost sent my husband back for my shawl!" Both the ladies laughed and acquired merit with each other by their common experience.

"Those fans do make a great difference in the climate," said the gentleman at the head of the table. "They ought to have them going there by that pillar, or else close the ports. They only let in heat."

They easily conformed to the American convention of jocosity in their talk ; it perhaps no more represents the individual mood than the convention of dulness among other people ; but it seemed to make the young man feel at home.

"Why, do you think it's uncomfortably warm?" he asked, from what March perceived to be a meteorology of his own. He laughed and added, "It *is* pretty summer-like," as if he had not thought of it before. He talked of the big mail-boat, and said he would like to cross on such a boat as that, and then he glanced at the possible advantage of having your own steam-yacht like the one which he said they had just passed, so near that you could see what a good time the people were having on board. He began to speak to the Marches ; his talk spread to the young couple across the table ; it visited the mother on the sofa in a remark which she might ignore without apparent rejection, and without really avoiding the boy, it glanced off towards the father and daughter, from whom it fell, to rest with the gentleman at the head of the table.

It was not that the father and daughter had slighted his overture, if it was so much as that, but that they were tacitly preoccupied, or were of some philosophy concerning their fellow-breakfasters which did not suffer them, for the present at least, to share in the common friend-liness. This is an attitude sometimes produced in people by a sense of just, or even unjust, superiority, sometimes by serious trouble; sometimes by transient annoyance. The cause was not so deep-seated but Mrs. March, before she rose from her place, believed that she had detected a slant of the young lady's eyes, from under her lashes, towards the young man ; and she leaped to a conclusion concerning them in a matter where all logical steps are impertinent. She did not announce her arrival at this point till the young man had overtaken her before she got out of the saloon, and presented the handkerchief she had dropped under the table.

He went away with her thanks, and then she said to her husband, "Well, he's perfectly charming, and I don't wonder she's taken with him; that kind of cold girl would be, though I'm not sure that she *is* cold. She's interesting, and you could see that he thought so, the more he looked at her; I could see him looking at her from the very first instant; he couldn't keep his eyes off her; she piqued his curiosity, and made him wonder about her."

"Now, look here, Isabel! This won't do. I can stand a good deal, but I sat between you and that young fellow, and you couldn't tell whether he was looking at that girl or not."

"I could! I could tell by the expression of her face."

"Oh, well! If it's gone as far as that with

you, I give it up. When are you going to have them married?"

"Nonsense! I want you to find out who *all* those people are. How are you going to do it?"

"Perhaps the passenger-list will say," he suggested.

VIII

THE list did not say of itself, but with the help of the head steward's diagram it said that the gentleman at the head of the table was Mr. R. M. Kenby; the father and the daughter were Mr. E. B. Triscoe and Miss Triscoe; the bridal pair were Mr. and Mrs. Leffers; the mother and her son were Mrs. Adding and Mr. Roswell Adding; the young man who came in last was Mr. L. J. Burnamy. March carried the list, with these names carefully checked and rearranged on a neat plan of the table, to his wife in her steamer chair, and left her to make out the history and the character of the people from it. In this sort of conjecture long experience had taught him his futility, and he strolled up and down and looked at the life about him with no wish to penetrate it deeply.

Long Island was now a low yellow line on

"LONG ISLAND WAS NOW A LOW YELLOW LINE"

the left. Some fishing-boats flickered off the shore; they met a few sail, and left more behind; but already, and so near one of the greatest ports of the world, the spacious solitude of the ocean was beginning. There was no swell; the sea lay quite flat, with a fine mesh of wrinkles on its surface, and the sun flamed down upon it from a sky without a cloud. With the light fair wind, there was no resistance in the sultry air; the thin, dun smoke from the smoke-stack fell about the decks like a stifling veil.

The promenades were as uncomfortably crowded as the sidewalk of Fourteenth Street on a summer's day, and showed much the social average of a New York shopping thoroughfare. Distinction is something that does not always reveal itself at first sight on land; and at sea it is still more retiring. A certain democracy of looks and clothes was the most notable thing to March in the apathetic groups and detached figures. His criticism disabled the saloon passengers of even so much personal appeal as he imagined in some of the second-cabin passengers whom he saw across their barrier; they had at least the pathos of their exclusion, and he could wonder if they felt it or envied him.

At Hoboken he had seen certain people coming on board who looked like swells; but they had now either retired from the crowd, or they had already conformed to the prevailing type. It was very well as a type ; he was of it himself ; but he wished that beauty as well as distinction had not been so lost in it.

In fact, he no longer saw so much beauty anywhere as he once did. It might be that he saw life more truly than when he was young, and that his glasses were better than his eyes had been ; but there were analogies that forbade his thinking so, and he sometimes had his misgivings that the trouble was with his glasses. He made what he could of a pretty girl who had the air of not meaning to lose a moment from flirtation, and was luring her fellow - passengers from under her sailor hat. She had already attached one of them, and she was looking out for more. She kept moving herself from the waist up, as if she worked there on a pivot, showing now this side and now that side of her face, and visiting the admirer she had secured with a smile as from the lamp of a revolving light as she turned.

While he was dwelling upon this folly, with a sense of impersonal pleasure in it as complete through his years as if he were already a disembodied spirit, the pulse of the engines suddenly ceased, and he joined the general rush to the rail, with a fantastic expectation of seeing another distracted mother put off ; but it was only the pilot leaving the ship. He was climbing down the ladder which hung over the

" THE SPACIOUS SOLITUDE OF THE OCEAN WAS BEGINNING "

boat, rising and sinking on the sea below, while the two men in her held her from the ship's side with their oars ; in the offing lay the white steam-yacht which now replaces the picturesque pilot - sloop of other times. The *Norumbia's* screws turned again under half a head of steam ; the pilot dropped from the last rung of the ladder into the boat, and caught the bundle of letters tossed after him. Then his men let go the line that was towing their craft, and the incident of the steamer's departure was finally closed. It had been dramatically heightened perhaps by her final impatience to be off at some added risk to the pilot and his men, but not painfully so, and March smiled to think how men whose lives are full of dangerous chances seem always to take as many of them as they can.

He heard a girl's fresh voice saying at his shoulder, "Well, now we *are* off ; and I suppose you're glad, papa?"

"I'm glad we're not taking the pilot *on*, at least," answered the elderly man whom the girl had spoken to ; and March turned to see the father and daughter whose reticence at the breakfast - table had interested him. He wondered that he had left her out of the account in estimating the beauty of the ship's passengers ; he saw now that she was not only extremely pretty, but as she moved away she was very graceful ; she even had distinction.

He had fancied a tone of tolerance and at the same time of reproach in her voice, when she spoke, and a tone of defiance and not very successful denial in her father's; and he went back with these impressions to his wife, whom he thought he ought to tell why the ship had stopped.

She had not noticed the ship's stopping, in her study of the passenger-list, and she did not care for the pilot's leaving; but she seemed to think his having overheard those words of the father and daughter an event of prime importance. With a woman's willingness to adapt the means to the end she suggested that he should follow them up and try to overhear something more; she only partially realized the infamy of her suggestion when he laughed in scornful refusal.

"Of course I don't want you to eavesdrop, but I *do* want you to find out about them. And about Mr. Burnamy, too. I can wait, about the others, or manage for myself, but these are driving me to distraction. Now, will you?"

He said he would do anything he could with honor, and at one of the earliest turns he made on the other side of the ship he was smilingly halted by Mr. Burnamy, who asked to be excused, and then asked if he were not Mr. March of *Every Other Week;* he had seen the name on the passenger-list, and felt sure it must be the editor's. He seemed so trustfully to expect March to remember his own name as that of a writer from whom he had accepted a short poem, yet unprinted, that the editor feigned to do so until he really did dimly recall it. He even recalled the short poem, and some civil words he said about it caused Burnamy to overrun in confidences that both touched and amused him.

IX

BURNAMY, it seemed, had taken passage on the *Norumbia* because he found, when he arrived in New York the day before, that she was the first boat out. His train was so much behind time that when he reached the office of the Hanseatic League it was nominally shut, but he pushed in by sufferance of the janitor, and found a berth which had just been given up, in one of the saloon-deck rooms. It was that or nothing ; and he felt rich enough to pay for it himself if the Bird of Prey, who had cabled him to come out to Carlsbad as his secretary, would not stand the difference between the price and that of the lower deck six-in-a-room berth which he would have taken if he had been allowed a choice.

With the three hundred dollars he had got for his book, less the price of his passage, changed into German bank-notes and gold pieces, and safely buttoned in the breast pocket of his waistcoat, he felt as safe from pillage as from poverty when he came out from buying his ticket; he covertly pressed his arm against his breast from time to time, for the joy of feeling his money there and not from any fear of finding it gone. He wanted to sing, he wanted to dance; he could not believe it was he, as he rode up the lonely length of Broadway in the cable-car, between the wild irregular walls of the canyon which the cable-cars have all to themselves at the end of a summer afternoon.

He went and dined, and he thought he dined well, at a Spanish-American restaurant, for fifty cents, with a half-bottle of California claret included. When he came back to Broadway he was aware that it was stiflingly hot in the pinkish twilight, but he took a cable-car again in lack of other pastime, and the motion served the purpose of a breeze, which he made the most of by keeping his hat off. It did not really matter to him whether it was hot or cool; he was imparadised in weather which had nothing to do with the temperature. Partly because he was born to such weather, in the gayety of soul which amused some people with him, and partly because the world was behaving as he had always expected, he was opulently content with the present moment. But he thought very tolerantly of the future, and he confirmed himself in the decision he had already made, to stick to Chicago when he came back to America. New York was very well, and he had no sentiment about Chicago ; but he had got a foothold there ; he had done better with an Eastern publisher, he believed, by hailing from the West, and he did not believe it would hurt him with the Eastern public to keep on hailing from the West.

He was glad of a chance to see Europe, but he did not mean to come home so dazzled as to see nothing else against the American sky. He fancied, for he really knew nothing, that it was the light of Europe, not its glare that he wanted, and he wanted it chiefly on his material, so as to see it more and more objectively. It was his power of detachment from this that had enabled him to do his sketches in the paper with such charm as to lure a cash proposition from a publisher when he put them together for a book, but he believed that his business faculty had much to do with his success ; and he was as proud of that as of the book itself. Perhaps he was not so very proud of the book ; he was at least not vain of it ; he could detach himself from his art as well as his material.

Like all literary temperaments he was of a certain hardness, in spite of the susceptibilities that could be used to give coloring to his work. He knew this well enough, but he believed that there were depths of unprofessional ten-

"BROADWAY . . . THE IRREGULAR WALLS OF THE CANYON"

derness in his nature. He was good to his mother, and he sent her money, and wrote to her in the little Indiana town where he had left her when he came to Chicago. After he got that invitation from the Bird of Prey, he explored his heart for some affection that he had not felt for him before, and he found a wish that his employer should not know it was he who had invented that nickname for him. He promptly avowed this in the newspaper office which formed one of the eyries of the Bird of Prey, and made the fellows promise not to give him away. He failed to move their imagination when he brought up as a reason for softening towards him that he was from Burnamy's own part of Indiana, and was a benefactor of Tippecanoe University, from which Burnamy was graduated. But they relished the cynicism of his attempt ; and they were glad of his good-luck, which he was getting square, and not rhomboid, as most people seem to get their luck. They liked him, and some of them liked him for his clean young life as well as for his cleverness. His life was known to be as clean as a girl's, and he looked like a girl with his sweet eyes, though he had rather more chin than most girls.

The conductor came to reverse his seat, and Burnamy told him he guessed he would ride back with him as far as the line to the Hoboken Ferry, if the conductor would put him off at the right place. It was nearly nine o'clock, and he thought he might as well be going over to the ship, where he had decided to pass the night. After he found her, and went on board, he was glad he had not gone sooner. A queasy odor of drainage stole up from the waters of the dock, and mixed with the rank, gross sweetness of the bags of beet-root sugar from the freight-steamers; there was a coming and going of carts and trucks on the wharf, and on the ship a rattling of chains and a clucking of pulleys, with sudden outbreaks and then sudden silences of trampling sea-boots. Burnamy looked into the dining-saloon and the music-room, with the notion of trying for some naps there; then he went to his state-room. His room-mate, whoever he was to be, had not come; he kicked off his shoes and threw off his coat and tumbled into his berth.

He meant to rest awhile, and then get up and spend the night in receiving impressions. He could not think of any one who had done the facts of the eve of sailing on an Atlantic liner. He thought he would use the material first in a letter to the paper and afterwards in a poem; but he found himself unable to grasp the notion of its essential relation to the choice between chicken croquettes and sweetbreads as entrées of the restaurant dinner where he had been offered neither; he knew that he had begun to dream, and that he must get up. He

A STATE-ROOM INTERIOR

was just going to get up, when he woke to a sense of freshness in the air, penetrating from the new day outside. He looked at his watch and found it was quarter past six ; he glanced round the state-room and saw that he had passed the night alone in it. Then he splashed himself hastily at the basin next his berth, and jumped into his clothes, and went on deck, anxious to lose no feature or emotion of the ship's departure.

When she was fairly off he returned to his room to change the thick coat he had put on at the instigation of the early morning air. His room-mate was still absent, but he was now represented by his state-room baggage, and Burnamy tried to infer him from it. He perceived a social quality in his dress-coat case, capacious gladstone, hat-box, rug, umbrella, and sole-leather steamer trunk which he could not attribute to his own equipment. The things were not so new as his ; they had an effect of polite experience, with a foreign registry and customs label on them here and there. They had been chosen with both taste and knowledge, and Burnamy would have said that they were certainly English things, if it had not been for the initials U. S. A. which followed the name of E. B. Triscoe on the end of the steamer trunk showing itself under the foot of the lower berth.

The lower berth had fallen to Burnamy

through the default of the passenger whose ticket he had got at the last hour ; the clerk in the steamer office had been careful to impress him with this advantage, and he now imagined a trespass on his property. But he reassured himself by a glance at his ticket, and went out to watch the ship's passage down the stream and through the Narrows. After breakfast he came to his room again, to see what could be done from his valise to make him look better in the eyes of a girl whom he had seen across the table ; of course he professed a much more general purpose. He blamed himself for not having got at least a pair of the white tennis-shoes which so many of the passengers were wearing ; his russet shoes had turned shabby on his feet ; but there was a pair of enamelled leather boots in his bag which he thought might do.

His room was in the group of cabins on the upper deck ; he had already missed his way to it by mistaking the corridor which it opened into ; and he was not sure that he was not blundering again when he peered down the narrow passage where he supposed it was. A lady was standing at an open state-room door, resting her hands against the jambs and leaning forward with her head within and talking to some one there. Before he could draw back and try another corridor he heard her say: "Perhaps he's some young man, and wouldn't care."

Burnamy could not make out the answer which came from within. The lady spoke again in a tone of reluctant assent : " No, I don't suppose you could ; but if he understood, perhaps he would *offer*."

She drew her head out of the room, stepping back a pace, and lingering a moment at the threshold. She looked round over her shoulder and discovered Burnamy, where he stood hesitating at the head of the passage. She ebbed before him, and then flowed round him in her instant escape ; with some murmured incoherencies about speaking to her father, she vanished in a corridor on the other side of the ship, while he stood staring into the doorway of his room.

He had seen that she was the young lady for whom he had come to put on his enamelled shoes, and he saw that the person within was the elderly gentleman who had sat next her at breakfast. He begged his pardon, as he entered, and said he hoped he should not disturb him. " I'm afraid I left my things all over the place when I got up this morning."

The other entreated him not to mention it, and went on taking from his hand-bag a variety of toilet appliances which the sight of made Burnamy vow to keep his own simple combs and brushes shut in his valise all the way over. " You slept on board, then," he suggested, arresting himself with a pair of low

79

shoes in his hand ; he decided to put them in a certain pocket of his steamer-bag.

"Oh yes," Burnamy laughed, nervously : "I came near oversleeping, and getting off to sea without knowing it ; and I rushed out to save myself, and so—"

He began to gather up his belongings while he followed the movements of Mr. Triscoe with a wistful eye. He would have liked to offer the lower berth to this senior of his, when he saw him arranging to take possession of the upper ; but he did not quite know how to manage it. He noticed that as the other moved about he limped slightly, unless it were rather a weary easing of his person from one limb to the other. He stooped to pull his trunk out from under the berth, and Burnamy sprang to help him.

"Let me get that out for you !" He caught it up and put it on the sofa under the port. "Is that where you want it?"

"Why, yes," the other assented. "You're very good," and as he took out his key to unlock the trunk he relented a little further to the intimacies of the situation. "Have you arranged with the bath-steward yet ? It's such a full boat."

"No, I haven't," said Burnamy, as if he had tried and failed ; till then he had not known that there was a bath-steward. "Shall I get him for you ?"

A CORRIDOR BETWEEN STATE-ROOMS

"No, no. Our bedroom-steward will send him, I dare say, thank you."

Mr. Triscoe had got his trunk open, and Burnamy had no longer an excuse for lingering. In his defeat concerning the bath-steward, as he felt it to be, he had not the courage, now, to offer the lower berth. He went away forgetting to change his shoes; but he came back, and as soon as he got the enamelled shoes on, and shut the shabby russet pair in his bag, he said, abruptly : "Mr. Triscoe, I wish you'd take the lower berth. I got it at the eleventh hour by some fellow's giving it up, and it isn't as if I'd bargained for it a month ago."

The elder man gave him one of his staccato glances in which Burnamy fancied suspicion and even resentment. But he said, after the moment of reflection which he gave himself, "Why, thank you, if you don't mind, really."

"Not at all!" cried the young man. "I should like the upper berth better. We'll have the steward change the sheets."

"Oh, I'll see that he does that," said Mr. Triscoe. "I couldn't allow you to take any trouble about it." He now looked as if he wished Burnamy would go, and leave him to his domestic arrangements.

X

IN telling about himself Burnamy only
touched upon the points which he believed would take his listener's intelligent
fancy, and he stopped so long before he had
tired him that March said he would like to
introduce him to his wife. He saw in the
agreeable young fellow an image of his own
youth, with some differences which, he was
willing to own, were to the young fellow's advantage. But they were both from the middle
West; in their native accent and their local
tradition they were the same; they were the
same in their aspirations; they were of one
blood in their literary impulse to externate
their thoughts and emotions.

Burnamy answered, with a glance at his enamelled shoes, that he would be delighted, and
when her husband brought him up to her, Mrs.
March said she was always glad to meet the

contributors to the magazine, and asked him whether he knew Mr. Kendricks, who was her favorite. Without giving him time to reply to a question that seemed to depress him, she said that she had a son who must be nearly his own age, and whom his father had left in charge of *Every Other Week* for the few months they were to be gone ; that they had a daughter married and living in Chicago. She made him sit down by her in March's chair, and before he left them March heard him magnanimously asking whether Mr. Kendricks was going to do something more for the magazine soon. He sauntered away and did not know how quickly Burnamy left this question to say, with the laugh and blush which became him in her eyes :

"Mrs. March, there is something I should tell you about, if you will let me."

"Why, certainly, Mr. Burnamy," she began, but she saw that he did not wish her to continue.

"Because," he went on, "it's a little matter that I shouldn't like to go wrong in."

He told her of his having overheard what Miss Triscoe had said to her father, and his belief that she was talking about the lower berth. He said he would have wished to offer it, of course, but now he was afraid they might think he had overheard them and felt obliged to do it.

"I see," said Mrs. March, and she added, thoughtfully, "She looks like rather a proud girl."

"Yes," the young fellow sighed.

"She is very charming," she continued, thoughtfully, but not so judicially.

"Well," Burnamy owned, "that is certainly one of the complications," and they laughed together.

She stopped herself after saying, "I see what you mean," and suggested, "I think I should be guided by circumstances. It needn't be done at once, I suppose."

"Well," Burnamy began, and then he broke out, with a laugh of embarrassment, "I've done it already."

"Oh! Then it wasn't my *advice* exactly that you wanted."

"No"—

"And how did he take it?"

"He said he should be glad to make the exchange, if I really didn't mind." Burnamy had risen restlessly, and she did not ask him to stay. She merely said:

"Oh, well, I'm glad it turned out so nicely."

"I'm so glad you think it was the thing to do." He managed to laugh again, but he could not hide from her that he was not feeling altogether satisfied. "Would you like me to send Mr. March, if I see him?" he asked, as if he did not know on what other terms to get away.

"Do, please!" she entreated, and it seemed to her that he had hardly left her when her husband came up. "Why, where in the world did he find you so soon?"

"Did you send him for me? I was just hanging round for him to go." March sank into the chair at her side. "Well, is he going to marry her?"

"Oh, you may laugh! But there is something very exciting." She told him what had happened, and of her belief that Burnamy's handsome behavior had somehow not been met in kind.

March gave himself the pleasure of an immense laugh. "It seems to me that this Mr. Burnamy of yours wanted a little more gratitude than he was entitled to. Why shouldn't he have offered him the lower berth? And why shouldn't the old gentleman have taken it just as he did? Did you want him to make a counter offer of his daughter's hand? If he does, I hope Mr. Burnamy won't come for your advice till after he's accepted her."

"He *wasn't* very candid I hoped you would speak about that. Don't you think it was rather natural, though?"

"For him, very likely. But I think you would call it sinuous in some one you hadn't taken a fancy to."

"No, no. I wish to be just. I don't see how he could have come straight at it. And he did

own up at last." She asked him what Burnamy had done for the magazine, and he could
remember nothing but that one small poem,
yet unprinted ; he was rather vague about its
value, but said it had temperament.

"*He* has temperament, too," she commented,
and she had made him tell her everything
he knew, or could be forced to imagine about
Burnamy, before she let the talk turn to other
things.

The life of the promenade had already settled
into seafaring form ; the steamer chairs were
full, and people were reading or dozing in them
with an effect of long habit. Those who would
be walking up and down had begun their
walks ; some had begun going in and out of
the smoking-room ; ladies who were easily affected by the motion were lying down in the
music-room. Groups of both sexes were standing at intervals along the rail, and the promenaders were obliged to double on a briefer
course or work slowly round them. Shuffle-
board parties at one point and ring-toss parties
at another were forming among the young
people. It was as lively and it was as dull as it
would be two thousand miles at sea. It was
not the least cooler, yet ; but if you sat still
you did not suffer.

In the prompt monotony the time was already passing swiftly. The deck - steward
seemed hardly to have been round with tea

and bouillon, and he had not yet gathered up
all the empty cups, when the horn for lunch
sounded. It was the youngest of the table-
stewards who gave the summons to meals ;
and wherever the pretty boy appeared with
his bugle, funny passengers gathered round
him to make him laugh, and stop him from
winding it. His part of the joke was to fulfil
his duty with gravity, and only to give way to
a smile of triumph as he walked off.

XI

AT lunch, in the faded excitement of their
first meeting, the people at the Marches'
table did not renew the premature in-
timacy of their breakfast talk. Mrs. March
went to lie down in her berth afterwards, and
March went on deck without her. He began to
walk to and from the barrier between the first
and second cabin promenades; lingering near
it, and musing pensively, for some of the people
beyond it looked as intelligent and as socially
acceptable, even to their clothes, as their pe-
cuniary betters of the saloon.

There were two women, a mother and daughter, whom he fancied to be teachers, by their
looks, going out for a little rest, or perhaps for
a little further study to fit them more perfectly for their work. They gazed wistfully across
at him whenever he came up to the barrier;
and he feigned a conversation with them and

tried to convince them that the stamp of inferiority which their poverty put upon them was just, or if not just, then inevitable. He argued with them that the sort of barrier which here prevented their being friends with him, if they wished it, ran invisibly through society everywhere; but he felt ashamed before their kind, patient, intelligent faces, and found himself wishing to excuse the fact he was defending. Was it any worse, he asked them, than their not being invited to the entertainments of people in upper Fifth Avenue? He made them own that if they were let across that barrier the whole second cabin would have a logical right to follow; and they were silenced. But they continued to gaze at him with their sincere, gentle eyes whenever he returned to that barrier in his walk, till he could bear it no longer, and strolled off towards the steerage.

There was more reason why the passengers there should be penned into a little space of their own in the sort of pit made by the narrowing deck at the bow. They seemed to be all foreigners, and if any had made their fortunes in our country they were hiding their prosperity in the return to their own. They could hardly have come to us more shabby and squalid than they were going away; but he thought their average less apathetic than that of the saloon passengers, as he leaned over the rail and looked down at them. Some one had brought out an electric battery, and the lump-ish boys and slattern girls were shouting and laughing as they writhed with the current. A young mother seated flat on the deck, with her bare feet stuck out, inattentively nursed her babe, while she laughed and shouted with the rest ; a man with his head tied in a shawl walked about the pen and smiled grotesquely with the well side of his toothache-swollen face. The owner of the battery carried it away, and a group of little children, with blue eyes and yellow hair, gathered in the space he had left, and looked up at a passenger eating some plums and cherries which he had brought from the luncheon table. He began to throw the fruit down to them, and the children scram-bled for it.

An elderly man, with a thin, grave, aquiline face, said, " I shouldn't want a child of mine down there."

" No," March responded, " it isn't quite what one would choose for one's own. It's astonish-ing, though, how we reconcile ourselves to it in the case of others."

" I suppose it's something we'll have to get used to on the other side," suggested the stranger.

" Well," answered March, " you have some opportunities to get used to it on this side, if you happen to live in New York," and he went on to speak of the raggedness which often penetrated the frontier of comfort where he lived in Stuyvesant Square, and which seemed as glad of largesse in food or money as this poverty of the steerage.

The other listened restively like a man whose ideals are disturbed. " I don't believe I should like to live in New York, much," he said, and March fancied that he wished to be asked where he did live. It appeared that he lived in Ohio, and he named his town ; he did not brag of it, but he said it suited him. He added that he had never expected to go to Europe, but that he had begun to run down lately, and his doctor thought he had better go out and try Carlsbad.

March said, to invite his further confidence, that this was exactly his own case. The Ohio man met the overture from a common invalidism as if it detracted from his own distinction ; and he turned to speak of the difficulty he had in arranging his affairs for leaving home. His heart opened a little with the word, and he said how comfortable he and his wife were in their house, and how much they both hated to shut it up. When March offered him his card, he said he had none of his own with him, but that his name was Eltwin. He betrayed a simple wish to have March realize the local importance he had left behind him ; and it was not hard to comply ; March saw a Grand Army button in the lapel of his coat, and he knew that he was in the presence of a veteran.

He tried to guess his rank, in telling his wife about him, when he went down to find her just before dinner, but he ended with a certain sense of affliction. " There are too many elderly invalids on this ship. I knock against people of my own age everywhere. Why aren't your youthful lovers more in evidence, my dear? I don't believe they are lovers, and I begin to doubt if they're young, even."

" It wasn't very satisfactory at lunch, certainly," she owned. " But I know it will be different at dinner." She was putting herself together after a nap that had made up for the lost sleep of the night before. " I want you to look very nice, dear. Shall you dress for dinner?" she asked her husband's image in the state-room glass, which she was preoccupying.

" I shall dress in my pea-jacket and sea-boots," it answered.

" I have heard they always dress for dinner on the big Cunard and White Star boats, when it's good weather," she went on, placidly. " I shouldn't want those people to think you were not up in the *convenances*."

They both knew that she meant the reticent father and daughter, and March flung out, " I shouldn't want them to think *you* weren't. There's such a thing as overdoing."

She attacked him at another point. " What

94

has annoyed you? What else have you been doing?"

"Nothing. I've been reading most of the afternoon."

"*The Maiden Knight?*"

This was the book which nearly everybody had brought on board. It was just out, and had caught an instant favor, which swelled later to a tidal wave. It depicted a heroic girl in every trying circumstance of mediæval life, and gratified the perennial passion of both sexes for historical romance, while it flattered woman's instinct of superiority by the celebration of her unintermitted triumphs, ending in a preposterous and wholly superfluous self-sacrifice.

March laughed for pleasure in her guess, and she pursued, "I suppose you didn't waste time looking if anybody had brought the last copy of *Every Other Week?*"

"Yes, I did; and I found the one you had left in your steamer chair—for advertising purposes, probably."

"Mr. Burnamy has another," she said. "I saw it sticking out of his pocket this morning."

"Oh yes. He told me he had got it on the train from Chicago to see if it had his poem in it. He's an ingenuous soul—in some ways."

"Well, that is the very reason why you ought to find out whether the men are going to dress, and let him know. He would never think of it himself."

"Neither would I," said her husband.

"Very well, if you wish to spoil his chance at the outset," she sighed.

She did not quite know whether to be glad or not that the men were all in sacks and cut-aways at dinner; it saved her from shame for her husband and Mr. Burnamy; but it put her in the wrong. Every one talked; even the father and daughter talked with each other, and at one moment Mrs. March could not be quite sure that the daughter had not looked at her when she spoke. She could not be mistaken in the remark which the father addressed to Burnamy, though it led to nothing.

XII

THE dinner was uncommonly good, as the first dinner out is apt to be ; and it went gayly on from soup to fruit, which was of the American abundance and variety, and as yet not of the veteran freshness imparted by the ice-closet. Everybody was eating it, when by a common consciousness they were aware of alien witnesses. They looked up as by a single impulse, and saw at the port the gaunt face of a steerage passenger staring down upon their luxury ; he held on his arm a child that shared his regard with yet hungrier eyes. A boy's nose showed itself as if tiptoed to the height of the man's elbow ; a young girl peered over his other arm.

The passengers glanced at one another : the two table-stewards, with their napkins in their hands, smiled vaguely, and made some indefinite movements.

The bachelor at the head of the table broke the spell. "I'm glad it didn't begin with the Little Neck clams!"

"Probably they only let them come for the dessert," March suggested.

The widow now followed the direction of the other eyes, and looked up over her shoulder; she gave a little cry, and shrank down. The young bride made her petted mouth, in appeal to the company; her husband looked severe, as if he were going to do something, but refrained, not to make a scene. The reticent father threw one of his staccato glances at the port, and Mrs. March was sure that she saw the daughter steal a look at Burnamy.

The young fellow laughed. "I don't suppose there's anything to be done about it, unless we passed out a plate."

Mr. Kenby shook his head. "It wouldn't do. We might send for the captain. Or the chief steward."

The faces at the port vanished. At other ports profiles passed and repassed, as if the steerage passengers had their promenade under them, but they paused no more.

The Marches went up to their steamer chairs, and from her exasperated nerves Mrs. March denounced the arrangement of the ship which had made such a cruel thing possible.

"Oh," he mocked, "they had probably had a good substantial meal of their own, and the scene of our banquet was of the quality of a picture, a purely æsthetic treat. But supposing it wasn't, we're doing something like it every day and every moment of our lives. The *Norumbia* is a piece of the whole world's civilization set afloat, and passing from shore to shore with unchanged classes and conditions. A ship's merely a small stage, where we're brought to close quarters with the daily drama of humanity."

"Well, then," she protested, "I don't like being brought to close quarters with the daily drama of humanity, as you call it. And I don't believe that the large English ships are built so that the steerage passengers can stare in at the saloon windows while one is eating; and I'm sorry we came on the *Norumbia*."

"Ah, you think the *Norumbia* doesn't hide anything," he began, and he was going to speak of the men in the furnace pits of the steamer, how they fed the fires in a welding heat, and as if they had perished in it crept out on the forecastle like blanched phantasms of toil; but she interposed in time.

"If there's anything worse, for pity's sake don't tell me."

He sat thinking how once the world had not seemed to have even death in it, and then how as he had grown older death had come into it more and more, and suffering was lurking everywhere, and could hardly be kept out of

99

sight.   He wondered if that young Burnamy now saw the world as he used to see it, a place for making verse and making love, and full of beauty of all kinds waiting to be fitted with phrases.   He had lived a happy life ; Burnamy would be lucky if he should live one half as happy ; and yet if he could show him his whole happy life, just as it had truly been, must not the young man shrink from such a picture of his future ?

"Say something !" said his wife.   "What are you thinking about ?"

"Oh, Burnamy," he answered, honestly enough.

"I was thinking about the children," she said.   "I am glad Bella didn't try to come from Chicago to see us off ; it would have been too silly ; she is getting to be very sensible.   I hope Tom won't take the covers off the furniture when he has fellows in to see him."

"Well, I want him to get all the comfort he can out of the place, even if the moths eat up every stick of furniture."

"Yes, so do I.   And of course you're wishing that you were there with him !"   March laughed, guiltily.   "Well, perhaps it *was* a crazy thing for us to start off alone for Europe, at our age."

"Nothing of the kind," he retorted in the necessity he perceived for staying her drooping spirits.   "I wouldn't be anywhere else on any account. Isn't it perfectly delicious? It puts me in mind of that night on the Lake Ontario boat, when we were starting for Montreal. There was the same sort of red sunset, and the air wasn't a bit softer than this."

He spoke of a night on their wedding-journey when they were still new enough from Europe to be comparing everything at home with things there.

"Well, perhaps we shall get into the spirit of it again," she said, and they talked a long time of the past.

All the mechanical noises were muffled in the dull air, and the wash of the ship's course through the waveless sea made itself pleasantly heard. In the offing a steamer homeward bound swam smoothly by, so close that her lights outlined her to the eye; she sent up some signal rockets that soared against the purple heaven in green and crimson, and spoke to the *Norumbia* in the mysterious mute phrases of ships that meet in the dark.

Mrs. March wondered what had become of Burnamy; the promenades were much freer now than they had been since the ship sailed; when she rose to go below, she caught sight of him walking the deck transversely with some lady. She clutched her husband's arm and stayed him in rich conjecture.

"Do you suppose he *can* have got her to walking with him already?"

They waited till Burnamy and his companion came in sight again. She was tilting forward, and turning from the waist, now to him and now from him.

"No ; it's that pivotal girl," said March ; and his wife said, "Well, I'm glad he won't be put down by them."

In the music-room sat the people she meant, and at the instant she passed on down the stairs, the daughter was saying to the father, "I don't see why you didn't tell me sooner, papa."

"It was such an unimportant matter that I didn't think to mention it. He offered it, and I took it ; that was all. What difference could it have made to you?"

"None. But one doesn't like to do any one an injustice."

"I didn't know you were thinking anything about it."

"No, of course not."

XIII

THE voyage of the *Norumbia* was one of
those which passengers say they have
never seen anything like, though for the
first two or three days out neither the doctor
nor the deck-steward could be got to prophesy
when the ship would be in. There was only
a day or two when it could really be called
rough, and the sea-sickness was confined to
those who seemed wilful sufferers ; they lay
on the cushioned benching around the stairs-
landings and subsisted on biscuit and beef-tea
without qualifying the monotonous well-being
of the other passengers, who passed without
noticing them.

The second morning there was rain, and the
air freshened, but the leaden sea lay level as before. The sun shone in the afternoon ; with
the sunset the fog came thick and white ; the
ship lowed dismally through the night ; from

the dense folds of the mist answering noises called back to her. Just before dark two men in a dory shouted up to her close under her bows, and then melted out of sight; when the dark fell the lights of fishing-schooners were seen, and their bells pealed; once loud cries from a vessel near at hand made themselves heard. Some people in the dining-saloon sang hymns; the smoking - room was dense with cigar fumes, and the card - players dealt their hands in an atmosphere emulous of the fog without.

The *Norumbia* was off the Banks, and the second day of fog was cold as if icebergs were haunting the opaque pallor around her. In the ranks of steamer chairs people lay like mummies in their dense wrappings; in the music-room the little children of travel discussed the different lines of steamers on which they had crossed, and babes of five and seven disputed about the motion on the Cunarders and White Stars; their nurses tried in vain to still them in behalf of older passengers trying to write letters there.

By the next morning the ship had run out of the fog, and people who could keep their feet said they were glad of the greater motion which they found beyond the Banks. They now talked of the heat of the first days out, and how much they had suffered; some who had passed the night on board before sailing tried

to impart a sense of their misery in trying to sleep.

A day or two later a storm struck the ship, and the sailors stretched canvas along the weather promenade and put up a sheathing of boards across the bow end to keep off the rain. Yet a day or two more and the sea had fallen again, and there was dancing on the widest space of the lee promenade.

The little events of the sea outside the steamer offered themselves in their poor variety. Once a ship in the offing, with all its square sails set, lifted them like three white towers from the deep. On the rim of the ocean the length of some westward liner blocked itself out against the horizon, and swiftly trailed its smoke out of sight. A few tramp steamers, lounging and lunging through the trough of the sea, were overtaken and left behind; an old brigantine passed so close that her rusty iron sides showed plain, and one could discern the faces of the people on board.

The steamer was oftenest without the sign of any life beyond her. One day a small bird beat the air with its little wings, under the roof of the promenade, and then flittered from sight over the surface of the waste; a school of porpoises, stiff and wooden in their rise, plunged clumsily from wave to wave. The deep itself had sometimes the unreality, the artificiality of the canvas sea of the theatre.

Commonly it was livid and cold in color ; but there was a morning when it was delicately misted, and where the mist left it clear, it was blue, and exquisitely iridescent under the pale sun ; the wrinkled waves were finely pitted by the falling spray. These were rare moments ; mostly, when it was not like painted canvas, it was hard like black rock, with surfaces of smooth cleavage. Where it met the sky it lay flat and motionless, or in the rougher weather carved itself along the horizon in successions of surges.

If the sun rose clear, it was overcast in a few hours ; then the clouds broke and let a little sunshine through, to close again before the dim evening thickened over the waters. Sometimes the moon looked through the ragged curtain of vapors ; one night it seemed to shine till morning, and shook a path of quick-silver from the horizon to the ship. Through every change, after she had left the fog behind, the steamer drove on with the pulse of her engines (that stopped no more than a man's heart stops) in a course which had nothing to mark it but the spread of the furrows from her sides, and the wake that foamed from her stern to the western verge of the sea.

The life of the ship, like the life of the sea, was a sodden monotony with certain events which were part of the monotony. In the morning the little steward's bugle called the

"STOOD IN THE WAY OF THOSE WALKING UP AND DOWN"

passengers from their dreams, and half an hour later called them to their breakfast, after such as chose had been served with coffee by their bedroom-stewards. Then they went on deck, where they read, or dozed in their chairs, or walked up and down, or stood in the way of those who were walking ; or played shuffle-board and ring-toss ; or smoked, and drank whiskey and aerated waters over their cards and papers in the smoking-room ; or wrote letters in the saloon or the music-room. At eleven o'clock they spoiled their appetites for lunch with tea or bouillon to the music of a band of second-cabin stewards ; at one, a single blast of the bugle called them to lunch, where they glutted themselves to the torpor from which they afterwards drowsed in their berths or chairs. They did the same things in the afternoon that they had done in the forenoon ; and at four o'clock the deck-stewards came round with their cups and saucers, and their plates of sandwiches, again to the music of the band. There were two bugle-calls for dinner, and after dinner some went early to bed, and some sat up late and had grills and toast. At twelve the lights were put out in the saloons and the smoking-rooms.

There were various smells which stored themselves up in the consciousness to remain lastingly relative to certain moments and places : a whiff of whiskey and tobacco that exhaled from the door of the smoking-room; the odor of oil and steam rising from the open skylights over the engine-room; the scent of stale bread about the doors of the dining-saloon.

The life was like the life at a sea-side hotel, only more monotonous. The walking was limited; the talk was the tentative talk of people aware that there was no refuge if they got tired of one another. The flirting, such as there was of it, must be carried on in the glare of the pervasive publicity; it must be crude and bold, or not be at all.

There seemed to be very little of it. There were not many young people on board of saloon quality, and these were mostly girls. The young men were mainly of the smoking-room sort; they seldom risked themselves among the steamer chairs. It was gayer in the second cabin, and gayer yet in the steerage, where robuster emotions were operated by the accordion. The passengers there danced to its music; they sang to it and laughed to it unabashed under the eyes of the first-cabin witnesses, clustered along the rail above the pit where they took their rude pleasures.

With March it came to his spending many hours of each long, swift day in his berth with a book under the convenient electric light. He was safe there from the acquaintances which constantly formed themselves only to fall into disintegration, and cling to him afterwards as inorganic particles of salutation, weather-guessing, and smoking-room gossip about the ship's run.

In the earliest hours of the voyage he thought that he saw some faces of the great world, the world of wealth and fashion ; but these afterwards vanished, and left him to wonder where they hid themselves. He did not meet them even in going to and from his meals ; he could only imagine them served in those palatial state-rooms whose interiors the stewards now and then rather obtruded upon the public. There were people whom he encountered in the promenades when he got up for the sunrise, and whom he never saw at other times ; at midnight he met men prowling in the dark whom he never met by day. But none of these were people of the great world. Before six o'clock they were sometimes second-cabin passengers, whose barrier was then lifted for a little while to give them the freedom of the saloon promenade.

From time to time he thought he would look up his Ohioan, and revive from a closer study of him his interest in the rare American who had never been to Europe. But the old man kept with his elderly wife, who had the effect of withholding him from March's advances. Young Mr. and Mrs. Leffers threw off more and more their disguise of a long-married pair, and became frankly bride and groom. They seldom talked with any one else, except at table; they walked up and down together, smiling into each other's faces; they sat side by side in their steamer chairs: one shawl covered them both, and there was reason to believe that they were holding each other's hands under it.

Mrs. Adding often took the chair beside Mrs. March when her husband was straying about the ship or reading in his berth; and the two ladies must have exchanged autobiographies, for Mrs. March was able to tell him just how long Mrs. Adding had been a widow, what her husband died of, and what had been done to save him; how she was now perfectly wrapped up in her boy, and was taking him abroad, with some notion of going to Switzerland, after the summer's travel, and settling down with him at school there. She and Mrs. March became great friends; and Rose, as his mother called him, attached himself reverently to March, not only as a celebrity of the first grade in his quality of editor of *Every Other Week*, but as a sage of wisdom and goodness with whom he must not lose the chance of counsel upon almost every hypothesis and exigency of life.

March could not bring himself to place Burnamy quite where he belonged in contemporary literature, when Rose put him very high in virtue of the poem which he heard Burnamy

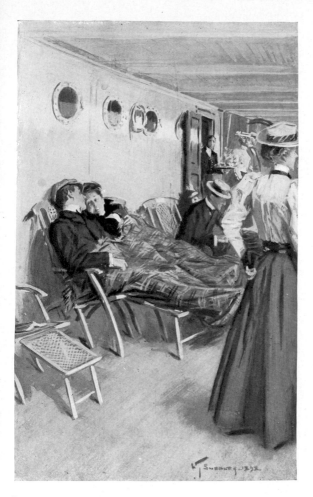

"THERE WAS EVERY REASON TO BELIEVE THAT THEY WERE
HOLDING EACH OTHER'S HAND"

was going to have printed in *Every Other Week*, and of the book which he was going to have published ; and he let the boy bring to the young fellow the flattery which can come to any author but once, in the first request for his autograph that Burnamy confessed to have had. They were so near in age, though they were ten years apart, that Rose stood much more in awe of Burnamy than of others much more his seniors. He was often in the company of Kenby, whom he valued next to March as a person acquainted with men ; he consulted March upon Kenby's practice of always taking up the language of the country he visited, if it were only for a fortnight; and he conceived a higher opinion of him for March's approval.

Burnamy was most with Mrs. March, who made him talk about himself when he supposed he was talking about literature, in the hope that she could get him to talk about the Triscoes ; but she listened in vain as he poured out his soul in theories of literary art, and in histories of what he had written and what he meant to write. When he passed them where they sat together, March heard the young fellow's perpetually recurring I, I, I, my, my, my, me, me, me ; and smiled to think how she was suffering under the drip-drip of his innocent egotism.

She bore in a sort of scientific patience with his attentions to the pivotal girl, and with Miss

Triscoe's indifference to him, in which a less penetrating scrutiny could have detected no change from meal to meal. It was only at table that she could see them together, or that she could note any break in the reserve of the father and daughter. The signs of this were so fine that when she reported them March laughed in scornful incredulity. But at breakfast the third day out, the Triscoes, with the authority of people accustomed to social consideration, suddenly turned to the Marches, and began to make themselves agreeable; the father spoke to March of *Every Other Week*, which he seemed to know of in its relation to him; and the young girl addressed herself to Mrs. March's motherly sense not the less acceptably because indirectly. She spoke of going out with her father for an indefinite time, as if it were rather his wish than hers, and she made some inquiries about places in Germany: they had never been in Germany. They had some idea of Dresden; but the idea of Dresden with its American colony seemed rather tiresome; and did Mrs. March know anything about Weimar?

Mrs. March was obliged to say that she knew nothing about any place in Germany; and she explained perhaps too fully where and why she was going with her husband. She fancied a Boston note in that scorn for the tiresomeness of Dresden; but the girl's style was of

A DECK STEWARD

New York rather than of Boston, and her accent was not quite of either place. Mrs. March began to try the Triscoes in this place and in that, to divine them and to class them. She had decided from the first that they were society people, but they were cultivated beyond the average of the few swells whom she had met ; and there had been nothing offensive in their manner of holding themselves aloof from the other people at the table ; they had a right to do that if they chose.

When the young Lefferses came in to breakfast, the talk went on between these and the Marches ; the Triscoes presently left the table, and Mrs. March rose soon after, eager for that discussion of their behavior which March knew he would not be able to postpone. He agreed with her that they were society people, but she could not at once accept his theory that they had themselves been the objects of an advance from them because of their neutral literary quality, through which they were of no social world. Later she admitted this, as she said, for the sake of argument, though what she wanted him to see, now, was that this was all a step of the girl's towards finding out something about Burnamy.

The same afternoon, about the time the deck-steward was making his round with his cups, Miss Triscoe abruptly advanced upon her from a neighboring corner of the bulkhead, and asked, with the air of one accustomed to have her advances gratefully received, if she might sit by her. The girl took March's vacant chair, where she had her cup of bouillon, which she continued to hold untasted in her hand after the first sip. Mrs. March did the same with hers, and at the moment she had got very tired of doing it Burnamy came by, for the hundredth time that day, and gave her a hundredth bow with a hundredth smile. He perceived that she wished to get rid of her cup, and he sprang to her relief.

"May I take yours, too?" he said very passively to Miss Triscoe.

"You are very good," she answered, and gave it.

Mrs. March with a casual air suggested, "Do you know Mr. Burnamy, Miss Triscoe?" The girl said a few civil things, but Burnamy did not try to make talk with her while he remained a few moments before Mrs. March. The pivotal girl came in sight, tilting and turning in a rare moment of isolation at the corner of the music-room, and he bowed abruptly, and hurried off to join her.

Miss Triscoe did not linger ; she alleged the necessity of looking up her father, and went away with a smile so friendly that Mrs. March might easily have construed it to mean that no blame attached itself to her in Miss Triscoe's mind.

"Then you don't feel that it was a very distinct success?" her husband asked on his return.

"Not on the surface," she said.

"Better let ill enough alone," he advised.

She did not heed him. "All the same she cares for him. The very fact that she was so cold shows that."

"And do you think her being cold will make him care for her?"

"If she wants it to.

XIV

A T dinner that day the question of *The Maiden Knight* was debated among the noises and silences of the band. Young Mrs. Leffers had brought the book to the table with her ; she said she had not been able to lay it down before the last horn sounded ; in fact, she could have been seen reading it to her husband, where they sat under the same shawl, the whole afternoon. "Don't you think it's perfectly fascinating?" she asked Mrs. Adding, with her petted mouth.

"Well," said the widow, doubtfully, "it's nearly a week since I read it, and I've had time to get over the glow."

"Oh, I could just read it forever !" the bride exclaimed.

"I like a book," said her husband, "that takes me out of myself. I don't want to think when I'm reading."

March was going to attack this ideal, but he reflected in time that Mr. Leffers had really stated his own motive in reading. He compromised. "Well, I like the author to do my thinking for me."

"Yes," said the other, "that is what I mean."

"The question is whether *The Maiden Knight* fellow does it," said Kenby, taking duck and pease from the steward at his shoulder.

"What my wife likes in it is to see what one woman can do and be, single-handed," said March.

"No," his wife corrected him, "what a man thinks she can."

"I suppose," said Mr. Triscoe, unexpectedly, "that we're like the English in our habit of going off about a book like a train of powder."

"If you'll say a row of bricks," March assented, "I'll agree with you. It's certainly Anglo-Saxon to fall over one another as we do, when we get going. It would be interesting to know just how much liking there is in the popularity of a given book."

"It's like the run of a song, isn't it?" Kenby suggested. "You can't stand either when it reaches a given point."

He spoke to March and ignored Triscoe, who had hitherto ignored the rest of the table.

"It's very curious," March said. "The book or the song catches a mood, or feeds a craving, and when one passes or the other is glutted—"

"The discouraging part is," Triscoe put in, still limiting himself to the Marches, "that it's never a question of real taste. The things that go down with us are so crude, so coarsely spiced; they tickle such a vulgar palate— Now in France, for instance," he suggested.

"Well, I don't know," returned the editor. "After all, we eat a good deal of bread, and we drink more pure water than any other people. Even when we drink it iced, I fancy it isn't so bad as absinthe."

The young bride looked at him gratefully, but she said, "If we can't get ice-water in Europe, I don't know what Mr. Leffers *will* do," and the talk threatened to pass among the ladies into a comparison of American and European customs.

Burnamy could not bear to let it. "I don't pretend to be very well up in French literature," he began, "but I think such a book as *The Maiden Knight* isn't such a bad piece of work; people are liking a pretty well built story when they like it. Of course it's sentimental, and it begs the question a good deal; but it imagines something heroic in character, and it makes the reader imagine it too. The man who wrote that book may be a donkey half the time, but he's a genius the other half. By-and-by he'll do something—after he comes to see that his Maiden Knight was a fool—that I believe even you won't be down on, Mr. March, if he paints a heroic type as powerfully as he does in this book."

He spoke with the authority of a journalist, and though he deferred to March in the end, he deferred with authority still. March liked him for coming to the defence of the young writer whom he had not himself learned to like yet. "Yes," he said, "if he has the power you say, and can keep it after he comes to his artistic consciousness."

Mrs. Leffers, as if she thought things were going her way, smiled; Rose Adding listened with shining eyes expectantly fixed on March; his mother viewed his rapture with tender amusement. The steward was at Kenby's shoulder with the salad and his entreating "*Bleace!*" and Triscoe seemed to be questioning whether he should take any notice of Burnamy's general disagreement. He said at last: "I'm afraid we haven't the documents. You don't seem to have cared for French books, and I haven't read *The Maiden Knight.*" He added to March: "But I don't defend absinthe. Ice-water is better. What I object to is our indiscriminate taste both for raw whiskey and for milk-and-water."

No one took up the question again, and it was Kenby who spoke next. "The doctor thinks, if this weather holds, that we shall be into Plymouth Wednesday morning. I always like to get a professional opinion on the ship's run."

In the evening, as Mrs. March was putting away in her portfolio the journal-letter which she was writing to send back from Plymouth to her children, Miss Triscoe drifted to the place where she sat at their table in the dining-room by a coincidence which they both respected as casual.

"We had quite a literary dinner," she remarked, hovering for a moment near the chair which she later sank into. "It must have made you feel very much at home. Or perhaps you're so tired of it at home that you don't talk about books."

"We always talk shop, in some form or other," said Mrs. March. "My husband never tires of it. A good many of the contributors come to us, you know."

"It must be delightful," said the girl. She added as if she ought to excuse herself for neglecting an advantage that might have been hers if she had chosen, "I'm sorry one sees so little of the artistic and literary set. But New York is such a big place."

"New York people seem to be very fond of it," said Mrs. March. "Those who have always lived there."

"We haven't always lived there," said the girl. "But I think one has a good time there —the best time a girl can have. It's all very well coming over for the summer; one has to spend the summer somewhere. Are you going out for a long time?"

"Only for the summer. First to Carlsbad."

"Oh yes. I suppose we shall travel about through Germany, and then go to Paris. We always do; my father is very fond of it."

"You must know it very well," said Mrs. March, aimlessly.

"I was born there—if that means knowing it. I lived there till I was eleven years old. We came home after my mother died."

"Oh!" said Mrs. March.

The girl did not go further into her family history; but by one of those leaps which seem to women as logical as other progressions, she arrived at asking, "Is Mr. Burnamy one of the —contributors?"

Mrs. March laughed. "He is going to be, as soon as his poem is printed."

"Poem?"

"Yes. Mr. March thinks it's very nice."

"I thought he spoke very nicely about *The Maiden Knight*. And he has been very nice to papa. You know they have the same room."

"I think Mr. Burnamy told me," Mrs. March said.

The girl went on. "He had the lower berth, and he gave it to papa; he's done everything but turn himself out of doors."

"I'm sure he's been very glad," Mrs. March

ventured on Burnamy's behalf, but very softly, lest if she breathed upon these budding
confidences they should shrink and wither
away.

"I always tell papa that there's no country
like America for real unselfishness; and if
they're all like *that*, in Chicago!" The girl
stopped, and added with a laugh, "But I'm
always quarrelling with papa about America."

"I have a daughter living in Chicago," said
Mrs. March, alluringly.

But Miss Triscoe refused the bait, either because she had said all she meant, or because
she had said all she would, about Chicago,
which Mrs. March felt for the present to be
one with Burnamy. She gave another of her
leaps. "I don't see why people are so anxious
to get it like Europe, at home. They say that
there was a time when there were no chaperons—before hoops, you know." She looked
suggestively at Mrs. March, resting one slim
hand on the table, and controlling her skirt
with the other, as if she were getting ready to
rise at any moment. "When they used to sit
on their steps."

"It was very pleasant before hoops—in every
way," said Mrs. March. "I was young, then;
and I lived in Boston, where I suppose it was
always simpler than in New York. I used to
sit on our steps. It was delightful for girls—
the freedom."

"I wish I had lived before hoops," said Miss Triscoe.

"Well, there must be places where it's before hoops yet : Seattle, and Portland, Oregon, for all I know," Mrs. March suggested. "And there must be people in that epoch everywhere."

"Like that young lady who twists and turns?" said Miss Triscoe, giving first one side of her face and then the other. "They have a good time. I suppose if Europe came to us in one way it had to come in another. If it came in galleries and all that sort of thing, it had to come in chaperons. You'll think I'm a great extremist, Mrs. March ; but sometimes I wish there was more America instead of less. I don't believe it's as bad as people say. Does Mr. March," she asked, taking hold of the chair with one hand, to secure her footing from any caprice of the sea, while she gathered her skirt more firmly into the other, as she rose, "does *he* think that America is going all wrong?"

"All wrong? How?"

"Oh, in politics, don't you know. And government, and all that. And bribing. And the lower classes having everything their own way. And the horrid newspapers. And everything getting so expensive ; and no regard for family, or anything of that kind."

Mrs. March thought she saw what Miss Triscoe meant, but she answered, still cautiously, "I don't believe he does always. Though there are times when he is very much disgusted. Then he says that he is getting too old—and we always quarrel about that—to see things as they really are. He says that if the world had been going the way that people over fifty have always thought it was going, it would have gone to smash in the time of the anthropoidal apes."

"Oh yes: Darwin," said Miss Triscoe, vaguely. "Well, I'm glad he doesn't give it up. I don't know but I was holding out just because I had argued so much, and was doing it out of—opposition. Good-night."

She called her salutation gayly over her shoulder, and Mrs. March watched her gliding out of the saloon with a graceful tilt to humor the slight roll of the ship, and a little lurch to correct it, once or twice, and wondered if Burnamy was afraid of her; it seemed to her that if she were a young man she should not be afraid of Miss Triscoe.

The next morning, just after she had arranged herself in her steamer chair, Burnamy approached her, bowing and smiling, with the first of his many bows and smiles for the day, and at the same time Miss Triscoe came towards her from the opposite direction. She nodded brightly to him, and he gave her a bow and smile, too; he always had so many of them to spare.

"Here is your chair!" Mrs. March called to her, drawing the shawl out of the chair next her own. "Mr. March is wandering about the ship somewhere."

"I'll keep it for him," said Miss Triscoe, and as Burnamy offered to take the shawl that hung in the hollow of her arm, she let it slip into his hand with an "Oh, thank you," which seemed also a permission for him to wrap it about her in the chair.

He stood talking before the ladies, but he looked up and down the promenade. The pivotal girl showed herself at the corner of the music-room, as she had done the day before. At first she revolved there as if she were shedding her light on some one hidden round the corner; then she moved a few paces farther out and showed herself more obviously alone. Clearly she was there for Burnamy to come and walk with her; Mrs. March could see that, and she felt that Miss Triscoe saw it too. She waited for her to dismiss him to his flirtation; but Miss Triscoe kept chatting on, and he kept answering, and making no motion to get away. Mrs. March began to be as sorry for her as she was ashamed for him. Then she heard him saying, "Would you like a turn or two?" and Miss Triscoe answering, "Why, yes, thank you," and promptly getting out of her chair as if the pains they had both been at to get her settled in it were all nothing.

She had the composure to say, "You can leave your shawl with me, Miss Triscoe," and to receive her fervent "Oh, *thank* you," before they sailed off together, with an inhuman indifference to the girl at the corner of the music-room. Then she sank into a kind of triumphal collapse, from which she roused herself to point her husband to the chair beside her when he happened along.

He chose to be perverse about her romance. "Well, now, you had better let them alone. Remember Kendricks." He meant one of their young friends whose love-affair they had promoted till his happy marriage left them in lasting doubt of what they had done. "My sympathies are all with the pivotal girl. Hadn't she as much right to him, for the time being, or for good and all, as Miss Triscoe?"

"That depends upon what you think of Burnamy."

"Well, I don't like to see a girl have a young man snatched away from her just when she's made sure of him. How do you suppose she is feeling now?"

"She isn't feeling at all. She's letting her revolving light fall upon half a dozen other young men by this time, collectively or consecutively. All she wants to make sure of is that they're young men—or old ones, even."

March laughed, but not altogether at what

134

his wife said. "I've been having a little talk with Papa Triscoe, in the smoking-room."

"You smell like it," said his wife, not to seem too eager. "Well?"

"Well, Papa Triscoe seems to be in a pout. He doesn't think things are going as they should in America. He hasn't been consulted, or if he has, his opinion hasn't been acted upon."

"I think he's horrid," said Mrs. March. "Who *are* they?"

"I couldn't make out, and I couldn't ask. But I'll tell you what I think."

"What?"

"That there's no chance for Burnamy. He's taking his daughter out to marry her to a crowned head."

XV

IT was this afternoon that the dance took
place on the south promenade. Everybody
came and looked, and the circle around the
waltzers was three or four deep. Between the
surrounding heads and shoulders, the hats of
the young ladies wheeling and whirling, and
the faces of the men who were wheeling and
whirling them, rose and sank with the rhythm
of their steps. The space allotted to the dancing was walled to seaward with canvas, and
was prettily treated with German and American flags ; it was hard to go wrong with flags,
Miss Triscoe said, securing herself under Mrs.
March's wing.

Where they stood they could see Burnamy's
face, flashing and flushing in the dance ; at the
end of the first piece he came to them, and remained talking and laughing till the music began again.

"Don't you want to try it?" he asked abruptly of Miss Triscoe.

"Isn't it rather—public?" she asked back.

Mrs. March could feel the hand which the girl had put through her arm thrill with temptation ; but Burnamy could not.

"Perhaps it *is* rather obvious," he said, and he made a long glide over the deck to the feet of the pivotal girl, anticipating another young man who was rapidly advancing from the opposite quarter. The next moment her hat and his face showed themselves in the necessary proximity to each other within the circle.

"How well she dances !" said Miss Triscoe.

"Do you think so ? She looks as if she had been wound up and set going."

"She's very graceful," the girl persisted.

The day ended with an entertainment in the saloon for one of the marine charities which address themselves to the hearts and pockets of passengers on all steamers. There were recitations in English and German, and songs from several people who had kindly consented, and ever more piano performance. Most of those who took part were of the race gifted in art and finance ; its children excelled in the music, and its fathers counted the gate-money during the last half of the programme, with an audible clinking of the silver on the table before them.

Miss Triscoe was with her father, and Mrs.

March was herself chaperoned by Mr. Burnamy : her husband had refused to come to the entertainment. She hoped to leave Burnamy and Miss Triscoe together before the evening ended ; but Miss Triscoe merely stopped with her father, in quitting the saloon, to laugh at some features of the entertainment, as people who take no part in such things do ; Burnamy stood up to exchange some unimpassioned words with her, and then they said good-night.

The next morning, at five o'clock, the *Norumbia* came to anchor in the pretty harbor of Plymouth. In the cool early light the town lay distinct along the shore, quaint with its small English houses, and stately with some public edifices of unknown function on the uplands ; a country-seat of aristocratic aspect showed itself on one of the heights ; on another the tower of a country church peered over the tree-tops; there were lines of fortifications, as peaceful, at their distance, as the stone walls dividing the green fields. The very ironclads in the harbor close at hand contributed to the amiable gayety of the scene under the pale blue English sky, already broken with clouds from which the flush of the sunrise had not quite faded. The breath of the land came freshly out over the water; one could almost smell the grass and the leaves. Gulls wheeled and darted over the crisp water ; the tones of

the English voices on the tender were pleasant to the ear, as it fussed and scuffled to the ship's side. A few score of the passengers left her; with their baggage they formed picturesque groups on the tender's deck, and they set out for the shore waving their hands and their handkerchiefs to the friends they left clustered along the rail of the *Norumbia*. Mr. and Mrs. Leffers bade March farewell, in the final fondness inspired by his having coffee with them before they left the ship; they said they hated to leave.

The stop had roused everybody, and the breakfast-tables were promptly filled, except such as the passengers landing at Plymouth had vacated; these were stripped of their cloths, and the remaining commensals placed at others. The seats of the Lefferses were given to March's old Ohio friend and his wife. He tried to engage them in the talk which began to be general in the excitement of having touched land; but they shyly held aloof.

Some English newspapers had come aboard from the tug, and there was the usual good-natured adjustment of the American self-satisfaction, among those who had seen them, to the ever-surprising fact that our continent is apparently of no interest to Europe. There were some meagre New York stock-market quotations in the papers; a paragraph in fine print announced the lynching of a negro in

Alabama; another recorded a coal - mining strike in Pennsylvania.

"I always have to get used to it over again," said Kenby. "This is the twentieth time I have been across, and I'm just as much astonished as I was the first, to find out that they don't want to know anything about us over here."

"Oh," said March, "curiosity and the weather both come from the west. San Francisco wants to know about Denver, Denver about Chicago, Chicago about New York, and New York about London; but curiosity never travels the other way any more than a hot wave or a cold wave."

"Ah, but London doesn't care a rap about Vienna," said Kenby.

"Well, some pressures give out before they reach the coast, on our own side. It isn't an infallible analogy."

Triscoe was fiercely chewing a morsel, as if in haste to take part in the discussion. He gulped it, and broke out : "Why should they care for us, anyway?"

March lightly ventured, "Oh, men and brothers, you know."

"That isn't sufficient ground. The Chinese are men and brothers; so are the South-Americans and Central-Africans, and Hawaiians; but we're not impatient for the latest news about them. It's civilization that interests civilization."

"I hope that fact doesn't leave us out in the cold with the barbarians?" Burnamy put in, with a smile.

"Do you think we are civilized?" retorted the other.

"We have that superstition in Chicago," said Burnamy. He added, still smiling, "About the New Yorkers, I mean."

"You're more superstitious in Chicago than I supposed. New York is an anarchy, tempered by vigilance committees."

"Oh, I don't think you can say that," Kenby cheerfully protested, "since the Reformers came in. Look at our streets!"

"Yes, our streets are clean, for the time being, and when we look at them we think we have made a clean sweep in our manners and morals. But how long do you think it will be before Tammany will be in the saddle again?"

"Oh, never in the world!" said the optimistic head of the table.

"I wish I had your faith; or I should if I didn't feel that it is one of the things that help to perpetuate Tammanys with us. You will see *our* Tammany in power after the next election." Kenby laughed in a large-hearted incredulity; and his laugh was like fuel to the other's flame. "New York is politically a mediæval Italian republic, and it's morally a frontier mining town. Socially it's—" He stopped as if he could not say what.

"I think it's a place where you have a very nice time, papa," said his daughter, and Burnamy smiled with her; not because he knew anything about it.

Her father went on as if he had not heard her. "It's as vulgar and crude as money can make it. Nothing counts but money, and as soon as there's enough, it counts for everything. In less than a year you'll have Tammany in power; it won't be more than a year till you'll have it in society."

"Oh no! Oh no!" came from Kenby. He did not care much for society, but he vaguely respected it as the stronghold of the proprieties and the amenities.

"Isn't society a good place for Tammany to be in?" asked March in the pause Triscoe let follow upon Kenby's laugh.

"There's no reason why it shouldn't be. Society is as bad as all the rest of it. And what New York is, politically, morally, and socially, the whole country wishes to be and tries to be."

There was that measure of truth in the words which silences; no one could find just the terms of refutation.

"Well," said Kenby at last, "it's a good thing there are so many lines to Europe. We've still got the right to emigrate."

"Yes, but even there we don't escape the abuse of our infamous newspapers for exercising a man's right to live where he chooses. And there is no country in Europe—except Turkey, or Spain—that isn't a better home for an honest man than the United States."

The Ohioan had once before cleared his throat as if he were going to speak. Now, he leaned far enough forward to catch Triscoe's eye, and said, slowly and distinctly : "I don't know just what reason you have to feel as you do about the country. I feel differently about it myself—perhaps because I fought for it."

At first, the others were glad of this arrogance; it even seemed an answer; but Burnamy saw Miss Triscoe's cheek flush, and then he doubted its validity.

Triscoe nervously crushed a biscuit in his hand, as if to expend a violent impulse upon it. He said, coldly, "I was speaking from that stand-point."

The Ohioan shrank back in his seat, and March felt sorry for him, though he had put himself in the wrong. His old hand trembled beside his plate, and his head shook, while his lips formed silent words ; and his shy wife was sharing his pain and shame.

Kenby began to talk about the stop which the *Norumbia* was to make at Cherbourg, and about what hour the next day they should all be in Cuxhaven. Miss Triscoe said they had never come on the Hanseatic Line before, and asked several questions. Her father did not speak again, and after a little while he rose without waiting for her to make the move from table ; he had punctiliously deferred to her hitherto. Eltwin rose at the same time, and March feared that he might be going to provoke another defeat, in some way.

Eltwin lifted his voice, and said, trying to catch Triscoe's eye, "I think I ought to beg your pardon, sir. I *do* beg your pardon."

March perceived that Eltwin wished to make the offer of his reparation as distinct as his aggression had been ; and now he quaked for Triscoe, whose daughter he saw glance apprehensively at her father as she swayed aside to let the two men come together.

"That is all right, Colonel—"

"Major," Eltwin conscientiously interposed.

"Major," Triscoe bowed ; and he put out his hand and grasped the hand which had been tremulously rising towards him. "There can't be any doubt of what we did, no matter what we've got."

"No, no!" said the other, eagerly. "That was what I meant, sir. I don't think as you do ; but I believe that a man who helped to save the country has a right to think what he pleases about it."

Triscoe said, "That is all right, my dear sir. May I ask your regiment ?"

The Marches let the old fellows walk away together, followed by the wife of the one and the daughter of the other. They saw the young girl making some graceful overtures of speech to the elder woman as they went.

"That was rather fine, my dear," said Mrs. March.

"Well, I don't know. It was a little too dramatic, wasn't it? It wasn't what I should have expected of real life."

"Oh, you spoil everything! If *that's* the spirit you're going through Europe in !"

"It isn't. As soon as I touch European soil I shall reform."

XVI

THAT was not the first time General Triscoe had silenced question of his opinions with the argument he had used upon Eltwin, though he was seldom able to use it so aptly. He always found that people suffered his belief in our national degeneration much more readily when they knew that he had left a diplomatic position in Europe (he had gone abroad as secretary of a minor legation) to come home and fight for the Union. Some millions of other men had gone into the war from the varied motives which impelled men at that time ; but he was aware that he had distinction, as a man of property and a man of family, in doing so. His family had improved as time passed, and it was now so old that back of his grandfather it was lost in antiquity. This ancestor had retired from the sea and became a merchant in his native

Rhode Island port, where his son established himself as a physician, and married the daughter of a former slave-trader whose social position was the highest in the place ; Triscoe liked to mention his maternal grandfather when he wished a listener to realize just how anomalous his part in a war against slavery was ; it heightened the effect of his pose.

He fought gallantly through the war, and he was brevetted Brigadier-General at the close. With this honor, and with the wound which caused an almost imperceptible limp in his gait, he won the heart of a rich New York girl, and her father set him up in a business, which was not long in going to pieces in his hands. Then the young couple went to live in Paris, where their daughter was born, and where the mother died when the child was ten years old. A little later his father-in-law died, and Triscoe returned to New York, where he found the fortune which his daughter had inherited was much less than he somehow thought he had a right to expect.

The income from her fortune was enough to live on, and he did not go back to Paris, where, in fact, things were not so much to his mind under the Republic as they had been under the Second Empire. He was still willing to do something for his country, however, and he allowed his name to be used on a citizen's ticket in his district ; but his provision-man was sent to Congress instead. Then he retired to Rhode Island and attempted to convert his shore property into a watering-place ; but after being attractively plotted and laid out with streets and sidewalks, it allured no one to build on it except the birds and the chipmonks, and he came back to New York, where his daughter had remained at school.

One of her maternal aunts made her a coming-out tea, after she left school ; and she entered upon a series of dinners, dances, theatre parties, and receptions of all kinds ; but the tide of fairy gold pouring through her fingers left no engagement-ring on them. She had no duties, but she seldom got out of humor with her pleasures ; she had some odd tastes of her own, and in a society where none but the most serious books were ever seriously mentioned she was rather fond of good ones, and had romantic ideas of a life that she vaguely called bohemian. Her character was never tested by anything more trying than the fear that her father might take her abroad to live ; he had taken her abroad several times for the summer.

The dreaded trial did not approach for several years after she had ceased to be a bud ; and then it came when her father was again willing to serve his country in diplomacy, either at The Hague, or at Brussels, or even at Berne. Reasons of political geography prevented his appointment anywhere, but General Triscoe having arranged his affairs for going abroad on the mission he had expected, decided to go without it. He was really very fit for both of the offices he had sought, and so far as a man can deserve public place by public service, he had deserved it. His pessimism was uncommonly well grounded, and if it did not go very deep, it might well have reached the bottom of his nature.

His daughter had begun to divine him at the early age when parents suppose themselves still to be mysteries to their children. She did not think it necessary ever to explain him to others ; perhaps she would not have found it possible ; and now after she parted with Mrs. Eltwin and went to sit down beside Mrs. March she did not refer to her father. She said how sweet she had found the old lady from Ohio ; and what sort of place did Mrs. March suppose it was where Mrs. Eltwin lived ? They seemed to have everything there, like any place. She had wanted to ask Mrs. Eltwin if they sat on their steps ; but she had not quite dared.

Burnamy came by, slowly, and at Mrs. March's suggestion he took one of the chairs on her other side, to help her and Miss Triscoe look at the Channel Islands and watch the approach of the steamer to Cherbourg, where the *Norumbia* was to land again. The young people talked across Mrs. March to each other,

151

and said how charming the islands were, in their gray-green insubstantiality, with valleys furrowing them far inward, like airy clefts in low banks of clouds. It seemed all the nicer not to know just which was which; but when the ship drew nearer to Cherbourg, he suggested that they could see better by going round to the other side of the ship. Miss Triscoe, as at the other times when she had gone off with Burnamy, marked her allegiance to Mrs. March by leaving a wrap with her.

Every one was restless in breaking with the old life at sea. There had been an equal unrest when the ship first sailed; people had first come aboard in the demoralization of severing their ties with home, and they shrank from forming others. Then the charm of the idle, eventless life grew upon them, and united them in a fond reluctance from the inevitable end. Now that the beginning of the end had come, the pangs of disintegration were felt in all the once-repellent particles. Burnamy and Miss Triscoe, as they hung upon the rail, owned to each other that they hated to have the voyage over. They had liked leaving Plymouth and being at sea again; they wished that they need not be reminded of another debarkation by the energy of the crane in hoisting the Cherbourg baggage from the hold.

They approved of the picturesqueness of

"THEY OWNED TO EACH OTHER THAT THEY HATED TO HAVE
THE VOYAGE OVER"

three French vessels of war that passed, dragging their kraken shapes low through the level
water. At Cherbourg an emotional French
tender came out to the ship, very different in
her clamorous voices and excited figures from
the steady self-control of the English tender
at Plymouth ; and they thought the French
fortifications much more on show than the
English had been. Nothing marked their
youthful date so much to the Marches, who
presently joined them, as their failure to realize that in this peaceful sea the great battle
between the *Kearsarge* and the *Alabama* was
fought. The elder couple tried to affect their
imaginations with the fact which reanimated
the spectre of a dreadful war for themselves ;
but they had to pass on and leave the young
people unmoved.

Mrs. March wondered if they noticed the
debarkation of the pivotal girl, whom she saw
standing on the deck of the tender, with her
hands at her waist, and giving now this side
and now that side of her face to the young
men waving their hats to her from the rail of
the ship. Burnamy was not of their number,
and he seemed not to know that the girl was
leaving him finally to Miss Triscoe. If Miss
Triscoe knew it she did nothing the whole
of that long, last afternoon to profit by the
fact. Burnamy spent a great part of it in
the chair beside Mrs. March, and he showed

155

an intolerable resignation to the girl's absence.

"Yes," said March, taking the place Burnamy left at last, "that terrible patience of youth!"

"Patience? Folly! Stupidity! They ought to be together every instant! Do they suppose that life is *full* of such chances? Do they think that fate has nothing to do but—"

She stopped for a fit climax, and he proposed, "Hang round and wait on them?"

"Yes! It's their one chance in a lifetime, probably."

"Then you've quite decided that they're in love?" He sank comfortably back, and put up his weary legs on the chair's extension with the conviction that love had no such joy as that to offer.

"I've decided that they're intensely interested in each other."

"Then what more can we ask of them? And why do you care what they do or don't do with their chance? Why do you wish their love well, if it's that? Is marriage such a very certain good?"

"It isn't all that it might be, but it's all that there is. What would our lives have been without it?" she retorted.

"Oh, we should have got on. It's such a tremendous risk that we ought to go round begging people to think twice, to count a hundred, or a nonillion, before they fall in love to the marrying-point. I don't mind their flirting; that amuses them; but marrying is a different thing. I doubt if Papa Triscoe would take kindly to the notion of a son-in-law he hadn't selected himself, and his daughter doesn't strike me as a young lady who has any wisdom to throw away on a choice. She has her little charm; her little gift of beauty, of grace, of spirit, and the other things that go with her age and sex; but what could she do for a fellow like Burnamy, who has his way to make, who has the ladder of fame to climb, with an old mother at the bottom of it to look after? You wouldn't want him to have an eye on Miss Triscoe's money, even if she had money, and I doubt if she has much. It's all very pretty to have a girl like her fascinated with a youth of his simple traditions; though Burnamy isn't altogether pastoral in his ideals, and he looks forward to a place in the very world she belongs to. I don't think it's for us to promote the affair."

"Well, perhaps you're right," she sighed. "I will let them alone from this out. Thank goodness, I shall not have them under my eyes very long."

"Oh, I don't think there's any harm done *yet*," said her husband, with a laugh.

At dinner there seemed so little harm of the kind he meant that she suffered from an illogical disappointment. The young people got through the meal with no talk that seemed inductive; Burnamy left the table first, and Miss Triscoe bore his going without apparent discouragement; she kept on chatting with March till his wife took him away to their chairs on deck.

There were a few more ships in sight than there were in mid-ocean; but the late twilight thickened over the North Sea quite like the night after they left New York, except that it was colder; and their hearts turned to their children, who had been in abeyance for the week past, with a remorseful pang. "Well," she said, "I wish we were going to be in New York in the morning, instead of Hamburg."

"Oh no! oh no!" he protested. "Not so bad as that, my dear. This is the last night, and it's hard to manage, as the last night always is. I suppose the last night on earth—"

"Basil!" she implored.

"Well, I won't, then. But what I want is to see a Dutch lugger. I've never seen a Dutch lugger, and—"

She suddenly pressed his arm, and in obedience to the signal he was silent; though it seemed afterwards that he ought to have gone on talking as if he did not see Burnamy and Miss Triscoe swinging slowly by. They were walking close together, and she was leaning forward and looking up into his face while he talked.

"*Now*," Mrs. March whispered, long after they were out of hearing, "let us go instantly. I wouldn't for worlds have them see us here when they get round again. They would feel that they had to stop and speak, and that would spoil everything. Come!"

XVII

BURNAMY paused in a flow of autobiography, and modestly waited for Miss Triscoe's prompting. He had not to wait long.

"And then, how soon did you think of printing your things in a book?"

"Oh, about as soon as they began to take with the public."

"How could you tell that they were—taking?"

"They were copied into other papers, and people talked about them."

"And that was what made Mr. Stoller want you to be his secretary?"

"I don't believe it was. The theory in the office was that he didn't think much of them; but he knows that I can write short-hand, and put things into shape."

"What things?"

"Oh—ideas. He has a notion of trying to come forward in politics. He owns shares in everything but the United States Senate—gas, electricity, railroads, aldermen, newspapers—and now he would like some Senate. That's what I think."

She did not quite understand, and she was far from knowing that this cynic humor expressed a deadlier pessimism than her father's fiercest accusals of the country. "How fascinating it is!" she said, innocently. "And I suppose they all envy your coming out?"

"In the office?"

"Yes. *I* should envy *them—staying.*"

Burnamy laughed. "I don't believe they envy me. It won't be all roses for me—they know that. But they know that I can take care of myself if it isn't." He remembered something one of his friends in the office had said of the painful surprise the Bird of Prey would feel if he ever tried his beak on him in the belief that he was soft.

She abruptly left the mere personal question. "And which would you rather write : poems, or those kind of sketches?"

"I don't know," said Burnamy, willing to talk of himself on any terms. "I suppose that prose is the thing for our time, rather more ; but there are things that you can't say in prose. I used to write a great deal of verse in college ; but I didn't have much luck with

editors till Mr. March took this little piece for
Every Other Week."

"Little? I thought it was a long poem!"

Burnamy laughed at the notion. "It's only
eight lines."

"Oh!" said the girl. "What is it about?"

He yielded to the temptation with a weak-
ness which he found incredible in a person of
his make. "I can repeat it if you won't give
me away to Mrs. March."

"Oh, no indeed!" He said the lines over to
her very simply and well. "They are beautiful—beautiful!"

"Do you think so?" he gasped, in his joy at
her praise.

"Yes, lovely. Do you know, you are the
first literary man — the only literary man — I
ever talked with. They *must* go out—somewhere! Papa must meet them at his clubs.
But I never do; and so I'm making the most
of you."

"You can't make too much of me, Miss Triscoe," said Burnamy.

She would not mind his mocking. "That
day you spoke about *The Maiden Knight*, don't
you know, I had never heard any one talk about
books in that way. I didn't know you were an
author then."

"Well, I'm not much of an author now," he
said, cynically, to retrieve his folly in repeating
his poem to her.

164

"Oh, that will do for *you* to say. But I know what Mrs. March thinks."

He wished very much to know what Mrs. March thought, too ; *Every Other Week* was such a very good place that he could not con- scientiously neglect any means of having his work favorably considered there ; if Mrs. March's interest in it would act upon her hus- band, ought not he to know just how much she thought of him as a writer? "Did she like the poem?"

Miss Triscoe could not recall that Mrs. March had said anything about the poem, but she launched herself upon the general current of Mrs. March's liking for Burnamy. "But it wouldn't do to tell you all she said !" This was not what he hoped, but he was richly con- tent when she returned to his personal history. "And you didn't know any one when you went up to Chicago from—"

"Tippecanoe? Not exactly that. I wasn't acquainted with any one in the office, but they had printed some things of mine, and they were willing to let me try my hand. That was all I could ask."

"Of course ! You knew you could do the rest. Well, it is like a romance. A woman couldn't have such an adventure as that !" sighed the girl.

"But women do !" Burnamy retorted. "There is a girl writing on the paper now

—she's going to do the literary notices while I'm gone — who came to Chicago from Ann Arbor, with no more chance than I had, and who's made her way single-handed from interviewing up."

"Oh," said Miss Triscoe, with a distinct drop in her enthusiasm. "Is she nice?"

"She's mighty clever, and she's nice enough, too, though the kind of journalism that women do isn't the most dignified. And she's one of the best girls I know, with lots of sense."

"It must be very interesting," said Miss Triscoe, with little interest in the way she said it. "I suppose you're quite a little community by yourselves."

"On the paper?"

"Yes."

"Well, some of us know one another, in the office, but most of us don't. There's quite a regiment of people on a big paper. If you'd like to come out," Burnamy ventured, "perhaps you could get the Woman's Page to do."

"What's that?"

"Oh, fashion; and personal gossip about society leaders; and recipes for dishes and diseases; and correspondence on points of etiquette."

He expected her to shudder at the notion, but she merely asked, "Do women write it?"

He laughed reminiscently. "Well, not always. We had one man who used to do it beautifully — when he was sober. The department hasn't had any permanent head since."

He was sorry he had said this, but it did not seem to shock her, and no doubt she had not taken it in fully. She abruptly left the subject. "Do you know what time we really get in to-morrow?"

"About one, I believe—there's a consensus of stewards to that effect, anyway." After a pause he asked, "Are you likely to be in Carlsbad?"

"We are going to Dresden, first, I believe. Then we may go on down to Vienna. But nothing is settled yet."

"Are you going direct to Dresden?"

"I don't know. We may stay in Hamburg a day or two."

"I've got to go straight to Carlsbad. There's a sleeping-car that will get me there by morning : Mr. Stoller likes zeal. But I hope you'll let me be of use to you any way I can before we part to-morrow."

"You're very kind. You've been very good already—to papa." He protested that he had not been at all good. "But he's used to taking care of himself on the other side. Oh, it's *this* side, now !"

"So it is ! How strange that seems ! It's

actually Europe. But as long as we're at sea, we can't realize it. Don't you hate to have experiences slip through your fingers?"

"I don't know. A girl doesn't have many experiences of her own; they're always other people's."

This affected Burnamy as so profound that he did not question its truth. He only suggested, "Well, sometimes they *make* other people have the experiences."

Whether Miss Triscoe decided that this was too intimate or not she left the question. "Do you understand German?"

"A little. I studied it at college, and I've cultivated a sort of beer - garden German in Chicago. I can ask for things."

"I can't, except in French, and that's worse than English, in Germany, I hear."

"Then you must let me be your interpreter up to the last moment. Will you?"

She did not answer. "It must be rather late, isn't it?" she asked. He let her see his watch, and she said, "Yes, it's very late," and led the way within. "I must look after my packing; papa's always so prompt, and I must justify myself for making him let me give up my maid when we left home; we expect to get one in Dresden. Good-night!"

Burnamy looked after her drifting down their corridor, and wondered whether it would have been a fit return for her expression of a sense of novelty in him as a literary man if he had told her that she was the first young lady he had known who had a maid. The fact awed him ; Miss Triscoe herself did not awe him so much.

XVIII

THE next morning was merely a transitional period, full of turmoil and disorder, between the broken life of the sea and the untried life of the shore. No one attempted to resume the routine of the voyage. People went and came between their rooms and the saloons and the decks, and were no longer careful to take their own steamer chairs when they sat down for a moment.

In the cabins the berths were not made up, and those who remained below had to sit on their hard edges, or on the sofas, which were cumbered with hand-bags and rolls of shawls. At an early hour after breakfast the bedroom stewards began to get the steamer trunks out and pile them in the corridors; the servants all became more caressingly attentive; and people who had left off settling the amount of the fees they were going to give, anxiously conferred together. The question whether you ought ever to give the head steward anything pressed crucially at the early lunch, and Kenby brought only a partial relief by saying that he always regarded the head steward as an officer of the ship. March made the experiment of offering him six marks, and the head steward took them quite as if he were not an officer of the ship. He also collected a handsome fee for the music, which is the tax levied on all German ships beyond the tolls exacted on the steamers of other nations.

After lunch the low, flat shore at Cuxhaven was so near that the summer cottages of the little watering-place showed through the warm drizzle much like the summer cottages of our own shore, and if it had not been for the strange, low sky, the Americans might easily have fancied themselves at home again.

Every one waited on foot while the tender came out into the stream where the *Norumbia* had dropped anchor. People who had brought their hand-baggage with them from their rooms looked so much safer with it that people who had left theirs to the stewards had to go back and pledge them afresh not to forget it. The tender came alongside, and the transfer of the heavy trunks began, but it seemed such an endless work that every one sat down in some other's chair. At last the trunks were all on the tender, and the bareheaded stewards began to run down the gangways with the hand-baggage. "Is this Hoboken?" March murmured in his wife's ear, with a bewildered sense of something in the scene like the reversed action of the kinematograph.

On the deck of the tender there was a brief moment of reunion among the companions of the voyage, the more intimate for their being crowded together under cover from the drizzle which now turned into a dashing rain. Burnamy's smile appeared, and then Mrs. March recognized Miss Triscoe and her father in their travel dress; they were not far from Burnamy's smile, but he seemed rather to have charge of the Eltwins, whom he was helping look after their bags and bundles. Rose Adding was talking with Kenby, and apparently asking his opinion of something; Mrs. Adding sat near them, tranquilly enjoying her son.

Mrs. March made her husband identify their baggage, large and small, and after he had satisfied her, he furtively satisfied himself by a fresh count that it was all there. But he need not have taken the trouble; their long, calm bedroom-steward was keeping guard over it; his eyes expressed a contemptuous pity for their anxiety, whose like he must have been very tired of. He brought their hand-bags into the customs-room at the station where they landed, and there took a last leave and a last fee with unexpected cordiality.

Again their companionship suffered eclipse in the distraction which the customs inspectors of all countries bring to travellers ; and again they were united during the long delay in the waiting-room, which was also the restaurant. It was full of strange noises and figures and odors—the shuffling of feet, the clash of crockery, the explosion of nervous German voices, mixed with the smell of beer and ham, and the smoke of cigars. Through it all pierced the wail of a postman standing at the door with a letter in his hand and calling out at regular intervals, "Krahnay, Krahnay !" When March could bear it no longer he went up to him and shouted, "Crane ! Crane !" and the man bowed gratefully, and began to cry, "Kren ! Kren !" But whether Mr. Crane got his letter or not, he never knew.

People were swarming at the window of the telegraph-office, and sending home cablegrams to announce their safe arrival ; March could not forbear cabling to his son, though he felt it absurd. There was a great deal of talking, but no laughing, except among the Americans, and the girls behind the bar who tried to understand what they wanted, and then served them with what they chose for them. Otherwise the Germans, though voluble, were unsmiling, and here on the threshold of their empire the travellers had their first hint of the anxious mood which seems habitual with these amiable people.

173

Mrs. Adding came screaming with glee to March where he sat with his wife, and leaned over her son to ask, "*Do* you know what lese-majesty is? Rose is afraid I've committed it!"

"No, I don't," said March. "But it's the unpardonable sin. What have you been doing?"

"I asked the official at the door when our train would start, and when he said at half-past three, I said, 'How tiresome!' Rose says the railroads belong to the state here, and that if I find fault with the time-table, it's constructive censure of the Emperor, and that's lese-majesty." She gave way to her mirth, while the boy studied March's face with an appealing smile.

"Well, I don't think you'll be arrested this time, Mrs. Adding; but I hope it will be a warning to Mrs. March. She's been complaining of the coffee."

"Indeed I shall say what I like," said Mrs. March. "I'm an American."

"Well, you'll find you're a German, if you like to say anything disagreeable about the coffee in the restaurant of the Emperor's railroad station; the first thing you know I shall be given three months on your account."

Mrs. Adding asked: "Then they won't punish ladies? There, Rose! *I'm* safe, you see;

and you're still a minor, though you *are* so wise for your years."

She went back to her table, where Kenby came and sat down by her.

"I don't know that I quite like her playing on that sensitive child," said Mrs. March. "And you've joined with her in her joking. Go and speak to him."

The boy was slowly following his mother, with his head fallen. March overtook him, and he started nervously at the touch of a hand on his shoulder, and then looked grate-fully up into the man's face. March tried to tell him what the crime of lese-majesty was, and he said: "Oh yes. I understood that. But I got to thinking; and I don't want my mother to take any risks."

"I don't believe she will, really, Rose. But I'll speak to her, and tell her she can't be too cautious."

"Not now, please," the boy entreated.

"Well, I'll find another chance," March assented. He looked round and caught a smil-ing nod from Burnamy, who was still with the Eltwins; the Triscoes were at a table by themselves; Miss Triscoe nodded too, but her father appeared not to see March. "It's all right with Rose," he said, when he sat down again by his wife; "but I guess it's all over with Burnamy," and he told her what he had seen. "Do you think it came to any displeasure between them last night? Do you suppose he offered himself, and she—"

"What nonsense!" said Mrs. March, but she was not at peace. "It's her father who's keeping her away from him."

"I shouldn't mind that. He's keeping her away from us, too." But at that moment Miss Triscoe, as if she had followed his return from afar, came over to speak to his wife. She said they were going on to Dresden that evening, and she was afraid they might have no chance to see each other on the train or in Hamburg. March, at this advance, went to speak with her father; he found him no more reconciled to Europe than America.

"They're Goths," he said of the Germans. "I could hardly get that stupid brute in the telegraph-office to take my despatch."

On his way back to his wife March met Miss Triscoe; he was not altogether surprised to meet Burnamy with her, now. The young fellow asked if he could be of any use to him, and then he said he would look him up in the train. He seemed in a hurry, but when he walked away with Miss Triscoe he did not seem in a hurry.

March remarked upon the change to his wife, and she sighed, "Yes, you can see that as far as *they're* concerned—"

"It's a great pity that there should be parents to complicate these affairs," he said.

"How simple it would be if there were no parties to them but the lovers! But nature is always insisting upon fathers and mothers, and families on both sides."

XIX

THE long train which they took at last
was for the *Norumbia's* people alone,
and it was of several transitional and
tentative types of cars. Some were still the
old coach-body carriages; but most were of a
strange corridor arrangement, with the aisle
at the side, and the seats crossing from it,
with compartments sometimes rising to the
roof, and sometimes rising half-way. No two
cars seemed quite alike, but all were very comfortable; and when the train began to run out
through the little sea-side town into the country, the old delight of strange travel began.
Most of the houses were little and low and
gray, with ivy or flowering vines covering
their walls to their brown-tiled roofs; there
was here and there a touch of Northern Gothic
in the architecture; but usually where it was
pretentious it was in the mansard taste, which

178

was so bad with us a generation ago, and is still very bad in Cuxhaven.

The fields, flat and wide, were dotted with familiar shapes of Holstein cattle, herded by little girls, with their hair in yellow pigtails. The gray, stormy sky hung low, and broke in fitful rains; but perhaps for the inclement season of mid-summer it was not very cold. Flowers were blooming along the embankments and in the rank green fields with a dogged energy; in the various distances were groups of trees embowering cottages and even villages, and always along the ditches and watercourses were double lines of low willows. At the first stop the train made, the passengers flocked to the refreshment-booth, prettily arranged beside the station, where the abundance of the cherries and strawberries gave proof that vegetation was in other respects superior to the elements. But it was not of the profusion of the sausages, and the ham which openly in slices or covertly in sandwiches claimed its primacy in the German affections; every form of it was flanked by tall glasses of beer.

A number of the natives stood by and stared unsmiling at the train, which had broken out in a rash of little American flags at every window. This boyish display, which must have made the Americans themselves laugh, if their sense of humor had not been lost in their impassioned patriotism, was the last expression of unity among the *Norumbia's* passengers, and they met no more in their sea-solidarity. Of their table acquaintances the Marches saw no one except Burnamy, who came through the train looking for them. He said he was in one of the rear cars with the Eltwins, and was going to Carlsbad with them in the sleeping-car train leaving Hamburg at seven. He owned to having seen the Triscoes since they had left Cuxhaven; Mrs. March would not suffer herself to ask him whether they were in the same carriage with the Eltwins. He had got a letter from Mr. Stoller at Cuxhaven, and he begged the Marches to let him engage rooms for them at the hotel where he was going to stay with his employer.

After they reached Hamburg they had flying glimpses of him and of others in the odious rivalry to get their baggage examined first which seized upon all, and in which they no longer knew each other, but selfishly struggled for the good-will of porters and inspectors. There was really no such haste; but none could govern themselves against the general frenzy. With the porter he secured March conspired and perspired to win the attention of a cold but not unkindly inspector. The officer opened one trunk, and after a glance at it marked all as passed, and then there ensued a heroic strife with the porter as to the pieces which were to

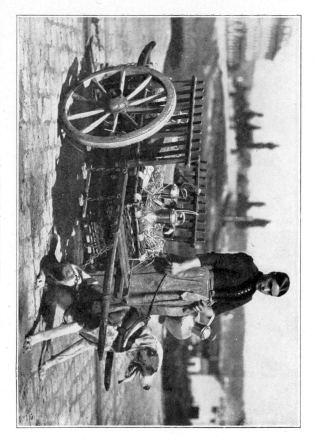

go to the Berlin station for their journey next day, and the pieces which were to go to the hotel overnight. At last the division was made ; the Marches got into a cab of the first class ; and the porter, crimson and steaming at every pore from the physical and intellectual strain, went back into the station.

They had got the number of their cab from the policeman who stands at the door of all large German stations and supplies the traveller with a metallic check for the sort of vehicle he demands. They were not proud, but it seemed best not to risk a second-class cab in a strange city, and when their first-class cab came creaking and limping out of the rank, they saw how wise they had been, if one of the second class could have been worse.

As they rattled away from the station they saw yet another kind of turnout, which they were destined to see more and more in the German lands. It was that team of a woman harnessed with a dog to a cart which the women of no other country can see without a sense of personal insult. March tried to take the humorous view, and complained that they had not been offered the choice of such an equipage by the policeman, but his wife would not be amused. She said that no place which suffered such a thing could be truly civilized, though he made her observe that no city in the world, except Boston or Brooklyn, was probably so thoroughly trolleyed as Hamburg. The hum of the electric car was everywhere, and everywhere the shriek of the wires overhead ; batlike flights of connecting plates traversed all the perspectives through which they drove to the pleasant little hotel they had chosen.

XX

ON one hand their windows gave upon
a basin of the Elbe, where stately white
swans were sailing; and on the other
to the new Rathhaus, over the trees that deeply
shaded the perennial mud of a cold, dim public
garden, where water-proof old women and im-
pervious nurses sat, and children played in the
long twilight of the sour, rain-soaked summer
of the father-land. It was all picturesque, and
within-doors there was the novelty of the
meagre carpets and stalwart furniture of the
Germans, and their beds, which after so many
ages of Anglo-Saxon satire remain immutably
preposterous. They are apparently imagined
for the stature of sleepers who have shortened
as they broadened; their pillows are trian-
gularly shaped to bring the chin tight upon
the breast under the bloated feather bulk
which is meant for covering, and which rises

over the sleeper from a thick substratum of cotton coverlet, neatly buttoned into the upper sheet, with the effect of a portly waistcoat.

The hotel was illumined by the kindly splendor of the uniformed *portier*, who had met the travellers at the door, like a glowing vision of the past, and a friendly air diffused itself through the whole house. At the dinner, which, if not so cheap as they had somehow hoped, was by no means bad, they took counsel with the English-speaking waiter as to what entertainment Hamburg could offer for the evening, and by the time they had drunk their coffee they had courage for the Circus Renz, which seemed to be all there was.

The conductor of the trolley-car, which they hailed at the street corner, stopped it and got off the platform, and stood in the street till they were safely aboard, without telling them to step lively, or pulling them up the steps, or knuckling them in the back to make them move forward. He let them get fairly seated before he started the car, and so lost the fun of seeing them lurch and stagger violently, and wildly clutch each other for support. The Germans have so little sense of humor that probably no one in the car would have been amused to see the strangers flung upon the floor. No one apparently found it droll that the conductor should touch his cap to them when he asked for their fare ; no one smiled at their efforts to make him understand where they wished to go, and he did not wink at the other passengers in trying to find out. Whenever the car stopped he descended first, and did not remount till the passenger had taken time to get well away from it. When the Marches got into the wrong car in coming home, and were carried beyond their street, the conductor would not take their fare.

The kindly civility which environed them went far to alleviate the inclemency of the climate; it began to rain as soon as they left the shelter of the car, but a citizen of whom they asked the nearest way to the Circus Renz was so anxious to have them go aright that they did not mind the wet, and the thought of his goodness embittered March's self-reproach for under-tipping the sort of gorgeous heyduk, with a staff like a drum-major's, who left his place at the circus door to get their tickets. He brought them back with a magnificent bow, and was then as visibly disappointed with the share of the change returned to him as a child would have been.

They went to their places with the sting of his disappointment rankling in their hearts. "One ought always to overpay them," March sighed, "and I will do it from this time forth ; we shall not be much the poorer for it. This heyduk is not going to get off with less than a mark when we come out." As an earnest of his good faith he gave the old man who showed them to their box a tip that made him bow double, and he bought every conceivable libretto and play - bill offered him at prices fixed by his remorse. "One ought to do it," he said. "We are of the quality of good geniuses to these poor souls ; we are Fortune—in disguise ; we are money found in the road. It is an accursed system, but they are more its victims than we." His wife quite agreed with him, and with the same good conscience between them they gave themselves up to the pure joy which the circus, of all modern entertainments, seems alone to inspire. The house was full from floor to roof when they came in, and every one was intent upon the two Spanish clowns, Lui-Lui and Soltamontes, whose drolleries spoke the universal language of circus humor, and needed no translation either into German or English. They had missed by an event or two the more patriotic attraction of "Miss Darlings, the american Star," as she was billed in English, but they were in good time for one of those equestrian performances which leave the spectator almost exanimate from their prolixity, and for the pantomimic piece which closed the evening.

This was not given until nearly the whole house had gone out and stayed itself with beer and cheese and ham and sausage, in the restaurant which purveys these light refresh-

HAMBURG RATHHAUS

ments in the summer theatres all over Germany. When the people came back gorged to the throat, they sat down in the right mood to enjoy the allegory of "the Enchantedmountain's Fantasy; the Mountainepisodes; the Highinteresting Sledges-Courses on the Steep Acclivities; the Amazing Uprush of the thence-plunging Four Trains, which arrive with Lightningsswiftness at the Top of the over-40-feet-high Mountain; the Highest Triumph of the To-day's Circus-Art; the Sledgejourney in the Wizardmountain, and the Fairy Ballet in the Realm of the Ghostprince, with Gold and Silver, Jewel, Bloomghosts, Gnomes, Gnomesses, and Dwarfs, in never-till-now-seen Splendor of Costume." The Marches were happy in this allegory, and happier in the ballet, which is everywhere delightfully innocent, and which here appealed with the large flat feet and the plain good faces of the *coryphées* to all that was simplest and sweetest in their natures. They could not have resisted, if they had wished, that environment of good-will; and if it had not been for the disappointed heyduk, they would have gone home from their evening at the Circus Renz without a pang.

They looked for him everywhere when they came out, but he had vanished, and they were left with a regret which if unavailing was not too poignant. In spite of it they had still an exhilaration in their release from the compan-

ionship of their fellow - voyagers, which they
analyzed as the psychical revulsion from the
strain of too great interest in them. Mrs.
March declared that for the present, at least,
she wanted Europe quite to themselves ; and
she said that not even for the pleasure of seeing Burnamy and Miss Triscoe come into their
box together would she have suffered an American trespass upon their exclusive possession of
the Circus Renz.

In the audience she had seen German officers
for the first time in Hamburg, and she meant,
if unremitting question could bring out the
truth, to know why she had not met any more.
She had read much of the prevalence and pre-
potence of the German officers who would try to
push her off the sidewalk, till they realized that
she was an American woman, and would then
submit to her inflexible purpose of holding it.
But she had been some seven or eight hours in
Hamburg, and nothing of the kind had happened to her, perhaps because she had hardly
yet walked a block in the city streets, but perhaps also because there seemed to be very few
officers or military of any kind in Hamburg.

XXI

THEIR absence was plausibly explained, the next morning, by the young German friend who came to see the Marches at breakfast. He said that Hamburg had been so long a free republic that the presence of a large imperial garrison was distasteful to the people, and as a matter of fact there were few soldiers quartered there, whether the authorities chose to indulge the popular grudge or not. He was himself in a joyful flutter of spirits, for he had just the day before got his release from military service. He gave them a notion of what the rapture of a man reprieved from death might be, and he was as radiantly happy in the ill health which had got him his release as if it had been the greatest blessing of heaven. He bubbled over with smiling regrets that he should be leaving his home for the first stage of the journey which he was to take in search of strength, and he pressed them to say if there was not something that he could do for them.

"Well," said Mrs. March, with a promptness surprising to her husband, who could think of nothing, "tell us where Heinrich Heine lived when he was in Hamburg. My husband has always had a great passion for him, and wants to look him up everywhere."

March had forgotten that Heine ever lived in Hamburg, and the young man had apparently never known it. His face fell; he wished to make Mrs. March believe that it was only Heine's uncle who had lived there; but she was firm; and when he had asked among the hotel people he came back gladly owning that he was wrong, and that the poet used to live in Königstrasse, which was very near by, and where they could easily know the house by his bust set in its front. The *portier* and the head waiter shared his ecstasy in so easily obliging the friendly American pair, and joined him in minutely instructing the driver when they shut them into their carriage.

They did not know that his was almost the only laughing face they should see in the serious German Empire; just as they did not know that it rained there every day. As they drove off in the gray drizzle with the unfounded hope that sooner or later the weather would be fine, they bade their driver be very

"HE BUBBLED OVER WITH SMILING REGRETS"

slow in taking them through Königstrasse, so that he should by no means miss Heine's dwelling, and he duly stopped in front of a house bearing the promised bust. They dismounted in order to revere it more at their ease, but the bust proved, by an irony bitterer than the sick, heart-breaking, brilliant Jew could have imagined in his cruelest moment, to be that of the German Milton, the respectable poet Klopstock, whom Heine abhorred and mocked so pitilessly.

In fact, it was here that the good, much-forgotten Klopstock dwelt, when he came home to live on a comfortable pension from the Danish government; and the pilgrims to the mistaken shrine went asking about among the neighbors in Königstrasse for some manner of house where Heine might have lived; they would have been willing to accept a flat, or any sort of two-pair back. The neighbors were somewhat moved by the anxiety of the strangers; but they were not so much moved as neighbors in Italy would have been. There was no eager and smiling sympathy in the little crowd that gathered to see what was going on; they were patient of question and kind in their helpless response, but they were not gay. To a man they had not heard of Heine; even the owner of a sausage and blood-pudding shop across the way had not heard of him; the clerk of a stationer-and-bookseller's next to the butcher's had heard of him, but he had never heard that he lived in Königstrasse ; he never had heard where he lived in Hamburg.

The pilgrims to the fraudulent shrine got back into their carriage, and drove sadly away, instructing their driver with the rigidity which their limited German favored not to let any house with a bust in its front escape him. He promised, and took his course out through Königstrasse, and suddenly they found themselves in a world of such eld and quaintness that they forgot Heine as completely as any of his countrymen had done. They were in steep and narrow streets, that crooked and turned with no apparent purpose of leading anywhere, among houses that looked down upon them with an astonished stare from the leaden-sashed windows of their timber-laced gables. The façades with their lattices stretching in bands quite across them, and with their steep roofs climbing high in successions of blinking dormers, were more richly mediæval than anything the travellers had ever dreamt of before, and they feasted themselves upon the unimagined picturesqueness with a leisurely minuteness which brought responsive gazers everywhere to the windows ; windows were set ajar ; shop doors were darkened by curious figures from within, and the traffic of the tortuous alleys was interrupted by their progress. They could not have said which delighted them

A STREET IN HAMBURG

more—the houses in the immediate foreground, or the sharp high gables in the perspectives and the background ; but all were like the painted scenes of the stage, and they had a pleasant difficulty in realizing that they were not persons in some romantic drama.

The illusion remained with them and qualified the impression which Hamburg made by her much-trolleyed Bostonian effect ; by the decorous activity and Parisian architecture of her business streets ; by the turmoil of her quays, and the innumerable masts and chimneys of her shipping. At the heart of all was that quaintness, that picturesqueness of the past, which embodied the spirit of the old Hanseatic city, and seemed the expression of the home-side of her history. The sense of this gained strength from such slight study of her annals as they afterwards made, and assisted the digestion of some of the toughest statistics. In the shadow of those Gothic houses the fact that Hamburg was one of the greatest coffee marts and money marts of the world had a romantic glamour ; and the fact that in the four years from 1870 till 1874 a quarter of a million emigrants sailed on her ships for the United States seemed to stretch a nerve of kindred feeling from those mediæval streets through the whole dreary length of Third Avenue.

It was perhaps in this glamour, or this feel-

ing of commercial solidarity, that March went
to have a look at the Hamburg Bourse, in the
beautiful new Rathhaus. It was not under-
going repairs, it was too new for that ; but it
was in construction, and so it fulfilled the function of a public edifice, in withholding its entire
interest from the stranger. He could not get
into the Senate-Chamber ; but the Bourse was
free to him, and when he stepped within, it rose
at him with a roar of voices and a sound of feet
like the New York Stock Exchange. The spectacle was not so frantic ; people were not shaking their fists or fingers in each other's noses ;
but they were all wild in the tamer German
way, and he was glad to mount from the Bourse
to the poor little art gallery up-stairs, and to
shut out its clamor. He was not so glad when
he looked round on these, his first examples
of modern German art. The custodian led him
gently about and said which things were for
sale, and it made his heart ache to see how bad
they were, and to think that, bad as they were,
he could not buy any of them.

XXII

IN the start from Cuxhaven the passengers
had the irresponsible ease of people ticket-
ed through, and the steamship company
had still the charge of their baggage. But
when the Marches left Hamburg for Leipsic
(where they had decided to break the long pull
to Carlsbad), all the anxieties of European travel, dimly remembered from former European
days, offered themselves for recognition. A
porter vanished with their hand-baggage before they could note any trait in him for iden-
tification ; other porters made away with their
trunks ; and the interpreter who helped March
buy his tickets, with a vocabulary of strictly
railroad English, had to help him find the pieces
in the baggage-room, curiously estranged in a
mountain of alien boxes. One official weighed
them ; another obliged him to pay as much in
freight as for a third passenger, and gave him

an illegible scrap of paper which recorded their number and destination. The interpreter and the porters took their fees with a professional effect of dissatisfaction. and he went to wait with his wife amidst the smoking and eating and drinking in the restaurant. They burst through with the rest when the doors were opened to the train, and followed a glimpse of the porter with their hand-bags, as he ran down the platform, still bent upon escaping them, and brought him to bay at last in a car where he had got very good seats for them, and sank into their places, hot and humiliated by their needless tumult.

As they cooled, they recovered their self-respect, and renewed a youthful joy in some of the long-estranged facts. The road was rougher than the roads at home ; but for much less money they had the comfort, without the unavailing splendor, of a Pullman in their second-class carriage. Mrs March had expected to be used with the severity on the imperial railroads which she had failed to experience from the military on the Hamburg sidewalks, but nothing could be kindlier than the whole management towards her. Her fellow-travellers were not lavish of their rights, as Americans are ; what they got, that they kept ; and in the run from Hamburg to Leipsic she had several occasions to observe that no German, however strong or robust, dreams of offering a better place, if he has one, to a lady in grace to her sex or age ; if they got into a carriage too late to secure a forward-looking seat, she rode backward to the end of that stage. But if they appealed to their fellow-travellers for information about changes, or stops, or any of the little facts that they wished to make sure of, they were enlightened past possibility of error. At the point where they might have gone wrong the explanations were renewed with a thoughtfulness which showed that their anxieties had not been forgotten. She said she could not see how any people could be both so selfish and so sweet, and her husband seized the advantage of saying something offensive :

"You women are so pampered in America that you are astonished when you are treated in Europe like the mere human beings you are."

She answered with unexpected reasonableness : "Yes, there's something in that ; but when the Germans have taught us how despicable we are as women, why do they treat us so well as human beings?"

This was at ten o'clock, after she had ridden backward a long way, and at last, within an hour of Leipsic, had got a seat confronting him. The darkness had now hidden the landscape, but the impression of its few simple elements lingered pleasantly in their sense ; long levels, densely wooded with the precise, severely disciplined German forests, and checkered with fields of grain and grass, soaking under the thin rain that from time to time varied the thin sunshine. The villages and peasants' cottages were notably few; but there was here and there a classic or a gothic villa, which, at one point, an English-speaking young lady turned from her Tauchnitz novel to explain as the seat of some country gentleman; the land was in large holdings, and this accounted for the sparsity of villages and cottages.

She then said that she was a German teacher of English, in Hamburg, and was going home to Potsdam for a visit. She seemed like a German girl out of *The Initials*, and in return for this favor Mrs. March tried to invest herself with some romantic interest as an American. She failed to move the girl's fancy, even after she had bestowed on her an immense bunch of roses which the young German friend in Hamburg had sent to them just before they left their hotel. She failed, later, on the same ground, with the pleasant-looking English woman who got into their carriage at Magdeburg, and talked over the London *Illustrated News* with an English-speaking Fräulein in her company; she readily accepted the fact of Mrs. March's nationality, but found nothing wonderful in it, apparently; and when she left the train she left Mrs. March to recall with fond regret the old days in Italy when she first came abroad, and could make a whole carriage full

of Italians break into ohs and ahs by saying that she was an American, and telling how far she had come across the sea.

"Yes," March assented, "but that was a great while ago, and Americans were much rarer than they are now in Europe. The Italians are so much more sympathetic than the Germans and English, and they saw that you wanted to impress them. Heaven knows how little they cared! And then, you were a very pretty young girl in those days; or at least I thought so."

"Yes," she sighed, "and now I'm a plain old woman."

"Oh, not quite so bad as that."

"Yes, I am! Do you think they would have cared more if it had been Miss Triscoe?"

"Not so much as if it had been the pivotal girl. They would have found *her* much more their ideal of the American woman; and even she would have had to have been here thirty years ago."

She laughed a little ruefully. "Well, at any rate, I should like to know how Miss Triscoe would have affected them."

"I should much rather know what sort of life that English woman is living here with her German husband; I fancied she had married rank. I could imagine how dull it must be in her little Saxon town from the way she clung to her *Illustrated News*, and explained the pictures of the royalties to her friend. *There* is romance for you !"

They arrived at Leipsic fresh and cheerful after their five hours' journey, and as in a spell of their travelled youth they drove up through the academic old town, asleep under its dimly clouded sky, and silent except for the trolley-cars that prowled its streets with their feline purr and broke at times into a long, shrill caterwaul. A sense of the past imparted itself to the well-known encounter with the porter and the head waiter at the hotel door, to the payment of the driver, to the endeavor of the secretary to have them take the most expensive rooms in the house, and to his compromise upon the next most, where they found themselves in great comfort, with electric lights and bells, and a quick succession of fee-taking callboys in dress-coats too large for them. The spell was deepened by the fact, which March kept at the bottom of his consciousness for the present, that one of their trunks was missing. This linked him the more closely to the travel of other days, and he spent the next forenoon in a telegraphic search for the estray, with emotions tinged by the melancholy of recollection, but in the security that since it was somewhere in the keeping of the state railway, it would be finally restored to him.

XXIII

THEIR windows, as they found in the morning, looked into a large square of aristocratic physiognomy, and of a Parisian effect in architecture, which afterwards proved characteristic of the town, if not quite so characteristic as to justify the passion of Leipsic for calling itself Little Paris. The prevailing tone was of a gray tending to the pale yellow of the Tauchnitz editions with which the place is more familiarly associated in the minds of English-speaking travellers. It was rather more sombre than it might have been if the weather had been fair ; but a quiet rain was falling dreamily that morning, and the square was provided with a fountain which continued to dribble in the rare moments when the rain forgot itself. The place was better shaded than need be in that sunless land by the German elms that look like ours, and it was sufficiently stocked

211

with German statues, that look like no others. It had a monument, too, of the kind with which German art has everywhere disfigured the kindly fatherland since the war with France. These monuments, though they are so very ugly, have a sort of pathos as records of the only war in which Germany unaided has triumphed against a foreign foe, but they are as tiresome as all such memorial pomps must be. It is not for the victories of a people that any other people can care. The wars come and go in blood and tears; but whether they are bad wars, or what are comically called good wars, they are of one effect in death and sorrow, and their fame is an offence to all men not concerned in them, till time has softened it to a memory

> "Of old, unhappy, far-off things,
> And battles long ago."

It was for some such reason that while the Marches turned with instant satiety from the swelling and strutting sculpture which celebrated the Leipsic heroes of the war of 1870, they had heart for those of the war of 1813; and after their noonday dinner they drove willingly, in a pause of the rain, out between yellowing harvests of wheat and oats to the field where Napoleon was beaten by the Russians, Austrians, and Prussians (it always took at least three nations to beat the little wretch)

SIEGESDENKMAL

fourscore years before. Yet even there Mrs. March was really more concerned for the sparsity of corn-flowers in the grain, which in their modern character of Kaiserblumen she found strangely absent from their loyal function ; and March was more taken with the notion of the little gardens which his guide told him the citizens could have in the suburbs of Leipsic and enjoy at any trolley - car distance from their homes. He saw certain of these gardens in groups, divided by low, unenvious fences, and sometimes furnished with summer-houses, where the tenant could take his pleasure in the evening air with his family. The guide said he had such a garden himself, at a rent of seven dollars a year, where he raised vegetables and flowers, and spent his peaceful leisure ; and March fancied that on the simple domestic side of their life, which this fact gave him a glimpse of, the Germans were much more engaging than in their character of victors over either the First or the Third Napoleon. But probably they would not have agreed with him, and probably nations will go on making themselves cruel and tiresome till humanity at last prevails over nationality.

He could have put the case to the guide himself ; but though the guide was imaginably liberated to a cosmopolitan conception of things by three years' service as waiter in English hotels, where he learned the language, he might

215

not have risen to this. He would have tried, for he was a willing and kindly soul, though he was not a *valet de place* by profession. There seemed, in fact, but one of that useless and amusing race (which is everywhere falling into decay through the rivalry of the perfected Baedekers) left in Leipsic, and this one was engaged, so that the Marches had to devolve upon their ex-waiter, who was now the keeper of a small restaurant. He gladly abandoned his business to the care of his wife, in order to drive handsomely about in his best clothes, with strangers who did not exact too much knowledge from him. In his zeal to do something he possessed himself of March's overcoat when they dismounted at their first gallery, and let fall from its pocket his prophylactic flask of brandy, which broke with a loud crash on the marble floor in the presence of several masterpieces, and perfumed the whole place. The masterpieces were some excellent works of Luke Kranach, who seemed the only German painter worth looking at when there were any Dutch or Italian pictures near, but the travellers forgot the name and nature of the Kranachs, and remembered afterwards only the shattered fragments of the brandy-flask, just how they looked on the floor, and the fumes, how they smelt, that rose from the ruin.

It might have been a warning protest of the veracities against what they were doing ; but

"THE SHATTERED FRAGMENTS OF THE BRANDY-FLASK"

the madness of sight-seeing, which spoils travel, was on them, and they delivered themselves up to it as they used in their ignorant youth, though now they knew its futility so well. They spared themselves nothing that they had time for that day, and they felt falsely guilty for their omissions, as if they really had been duties to art and history which must be discharged, like obligations to one's maker and one's neighbor.

They had a touch of genuine joy in the presence of the beautiful old Rathhaus, and they were sensible of something like a genuine emotion in passing the famous and venerable university ; the very air of Leipsic is redolent of printing and publication, which appealed to March in his quality of editor ; and they could not fail of an impression of the quiet beauty of the town, with its regular streets of houses breaking into suburban villas of an American sort, and intersected with many canals, which in the intervals of the rain were eagerly navigated by pleasure boats, and contributed to the general picturesqueness by their frequent bridges, even during the drizzle. There seemed to be no churches to do, and as it was a Sunday the galleries were so early closed against them that they were making a virtue as well as a pleasure of a visit to the famous scene of Napoleon's first great defeat.

By a concert between their guide and driver

their carriage drew up at the little inn by the road-side, which is also a museum stocked with relics from the battle-field, and with objects of interest relating to it. Old muskets, old swords, old shoes and old coats, trumpets, drums, gun-carriages, wheels, helmets, cannon-balls, grape-shot, and all the murderous rubbish which battles come to at last, with proclamations, autographs, caricatures and likenesses of Napoleon, and effigies of all the other generals engaged, and miniatures and jewels of their womenkind, filled room after room, through which their owner vaunted his way, with a loud, pounding voice and a bad breath. When he wishes them to enjoy some gross British satire or clumsy German gibe at Bonaparte's expense, and put his face close to begin the laugh, he was something so terrible that March left the place with a profound if not a reasoned regret that the French had not won the battle of Leipsic. He walked away musing pensively upon the traveller's inadequacy to the ethics of history when a breath could so sway him against his convictions; but even after he had cleansed his lungs with some deep respirations he found himself still a Bonapartist in the presence of that stone on the rising ground where Napoleon sat to watch the struggle on the vast plain, and see his empire slipping through his blood-stained fingers. It was with difficulty that he could keep from revering the

hat and coat which are sculptured on the stone, but it was well that he succeeded, for he could not make out then or afterwards whether the habiliments represented were really Napoleon's or not, and they might have turned out to be Barclay de Tolly's.

While he stood trying to solve this question of clothes he was startled by the apparition of a man climbing the little slope from the opposite quarter, and advancing towards them. He wore the imperial crossed by the pointed mustache once so familiar to a world much the worse for them, and March had the shiver of a weird moment in which he fancied the Third Napoleon rising to view the scene where the First had looked his coming ruin in the face.

"Why, it's Miss Triscoe!" cried his wife, and before March had noticed the approach of another figure, the elder and the younger lady rushed upon each other, and encountered with a kiss. At the same time the visage of the last Emperor resolved itself into the face of General Triscoe, who gave March his hand in a more tempered greeting. The ladies began asking each other of their lives since their parting two days before, and the men strolled a few paces away towards the distant prospect of Leipsic, which at that point silhouettes itself in a noble stretch of roofs and spires and towers against the horizon.

General Triscoe seemed no better satisfied

than he had been on first stepping ashore at
Cuxhaven. He might still have been in a pout
with his own country, but as yet he had not
made up with any other ; and he said, " What
a pity Napoleon didn't thrash the whole dun-
derheaded lot ! His empire would have been
a blessing to them, and they would have had
some chance of being civilized under the
French. All this unification of nationalities
is the great humbug of the century. Every
stupid race thinks it's happy because it's
united, and civilization has been set back a
hundred years by the wars that were fought
to bring the unions about, and more wars will
have to be fought to keep them up. What a
farce it is ! What's become of the nationality
of the Danes in Schleswig - Holstein, or the
French in the Rhine Provinces, or the Italians
in Savoy ?"

March had thought something like this himself, but to have it put by General Triscoe
made it offensive. " I don't know. Isn't it
rather quarrelling with the course of human
events to oppose accomplished facts ? The
unifications were bound to be, just as the sep-
arations before them were. And so far they
have made for peace, in Europe at least, and
peace is civilization. Perhaps after a great
many ages people will come together through
their real interests, the human interests ; but
at present it seems as if nothing but romantic

224

sentiment can unite them. By-and-by they may find that there is nothing in it ; but they will have to learn by experience."

"Perhaps," said the general, discontentedly. "I don't see much promise of any kind in the future."

"Well, I don't know. When you think of the solid militarism of Germany, you seem remanded to the most hopeless moment of the Roman Empire ; you think nothing can break such a force ; but my guide says that even in Leipsic the Socialists outnumber all the other parties, and the army is the great field of the Socialist propaganda. The army itself may be shaped into the means of democracy—even of peace."

"You're very optimistic," said Triscoe, curtly. "As I read the signs, we are not far from universal war. In less than a year we shall make the break ourselves in a war with Spain." He looked very fierce as he prophesied, and he dotted March over with his staccato glances.

"Well, I'll allow that if Tammany comes in this year, we shall have war with Spain. You can't ask more than that, General Triscoe ?"

Mrs. March and Miss Triscoe had not said a word of the battle of Leipsic, or of the impersonal interests which it suggested to the men. For all these, they might still have been sitting in their steamer chairs on the promenade of the *Norumbia* at a period which seemed now of

P   225

geological remoteness. The girl accounted for not being in Dresden by her father's having decided not to go through Berlin but to come by way of Leipsic, which he thought they had better see; they had come without stopping in Hamburg. They had not enjoyed Leipsic much; it had rained the whole day before, and they had not gone out. She asked when Mrs. March was going on to Carlsbad, and Mrs. March answered, the next morning; her husband wished to begin his cure at once.

Then Miss Triscoe pensively wondered if Carlsbad would do her father any good; and Mrs. March discreetly inquired General Triscoe's symptoms.

"Oh, he hasn't any. But I know he can't be well—with his gloomy opinions."

"*They* may come from his liver," said Mrs. March. "Nearly everything of that kind does. I know that Mr. March has been terribly depressed at times, and the doctor said it was *nothing* but his liver; and Carlsbad is the great place for *that*, you know."

"Perhaps I can get papa to run over some day, if he doesn't like Dresden. It isn't very far, is it?"

They referred to Mrs. March's Baedeker together, and found that it was five hours.

"Yes, that is what I thought," said Miss Triscoe, with a carelessness which convinced Mrs. March she had looked up the fact already.

"If you decide to come, you must let us get rooms for you at our hotel. We're going to Pupp's; most of the English and Americans go to the hotels on the Hill, but Pupp's is in the thick of it in the lower town; and it's very gay, Mr. Kenby says; he's been there often. Mr. Burnamy is to get our rooms."

"I don't suppose I can get papa to go," said Miss Triscoe, so insincerely that Mrs. March was sure she had talked over the different routes to Carlsbad with Burnamy — probably on the way from Cuxhaven. She looked up from digging the point of her umbrella in the ground. "You didn't meet him here this morning?"

Mrs. March governed herself to a calm which she respected in asking, "Has Mr. Burnamy been here?"

"He came on with Mr. and Mrs. Eltwin, when we did, and they all decided to stop over a day. They left on the twelve-o'clock train to-day."

Mrs. March perceived that the girl had decided not to let the facts betray themselves by chance, and she treated them as of no significance.

"No, we didn't see him," she said, carelessly.

The two men came walking slowly towards them, and Miss Triscoe said, "We're going to Dresden this evening, but I hope we shall meet somewhere, Mrs. March."

"Oh, people never lose sight of each other in Europe ; they can't ; it's so little !"

"Agatha," said the girl's father, "Mr. March tells me that the museum over there is worth seeing."

"Well," the girl assented, and she took a winning leave of the Marches, and moved gracefully away with her father.

"I should have thought it was Agnes," said Mrs. March, following them with her eyes before she turned upon her husband. "Did he tell you Burnamy had been here ? Well, he has ! He has just gone on to Carlsbad. He made those poor old Eltwins stop over with him, so he could be with *her*."

"Did she say that ?"

"No, but of course he did."

"Then it's all settled ?"

"No, it isn't settled. It's at the most interesting point."

"Well, don't read ahead. You always want to look at the last page."

"You were trying to look at the last page yourself," she retorted, and she would have liked to punish him for his complex dishonesty towards the affair ; but upon the whole she kept her temper with him, and she made him agree that Miss Triscoe's getting her father to Carlsbad was only a question of time.

They parted heart's-friends with their ineffectual guide, who was affectionately grateful

for the few marks they gave him, at the hotel door ; and they were in just the mood to hear men singing in a farther room when they went down to supper. The waiter, much distracted from their own service by his duties to it, told them it was the breakfast-party of students which they had heard beginning there about noon. The revellers had now been some six hours at table, and he said they might not rise before midnight ; they had just got to the toasts, which were apparently set to music.

The students of right remained a vivid color in the impression of the university town. They pervaded the place, and decorated it with their fantastic personal taste in coats and trousers, as well as their corps caps of green, white, red, and blue, but above all blue. They were not easily distinguishable from the bicyclers who were holding one of the dull festivals of their kind in Leipsic that day, and perhaps they were sometimes both students and bicyclers. As bicyclers they kept about in the rain, which they seemed not to mind ; so far from being disheartened, they had spirits enough to take one another by the waist at times and waltz in the square before the hotel. At one moment of the holiday some chiefs among them drove away in carriages ; at supper a winner of prizes sat covered with badges and medals ; another who went by the hotel streamed with ribbons : and an elderly man at his side was bespattered with small knots and ends of them, as if he had been in an explosion of ribbons somewhere. It seemed all to be as exciting for them, and it was as tedious for the witnesses, as any gala of students and bicyclers at home.

Mrs. March remained with an unrequited curiosity concerning their different colors and different caps, and she tried to make her husband find out what they severally meant ; he pretended a superior interest in the nature of a people who had such a passion for uniforms that they were not content with its gratification in their immense army, but indulged it in every pleasure and employment of civil life. He estimated, perhaps not very accurately, that only one man out of ten in Germany wore citizens' dress ; and of all functionaries he found that the dogs of the woman-and-dog teams alone had no distinctive dress ; even the women had their peasant costume.

There was an industrial fair open at Leipsic which they went out of the city to see after supper, along with a throng of Leipsickers, whom an hour's interval of fine weather tempted forth on the trolley ; and with the help of a little corporal, who took a fee for his service with the eagerness of a civilian, they got wheeled chairs, and renewed their associations with the great Chicago Fair in seeing the exposition from them. This was not, March said, quite the same as being drawn by a woman-and-dog team, which would have been the right means of doing a German fair; but it was something to have his chair pushed by a slender young girl, whose stalwart brother applied his strength to the chair of the lighter traveller; and it was fit that the girl should reckon the common hire, while the man took the common tip. They made haste to leave the useful aspects of the fair, and had themselves trundled away to the Colonial Exhibit, where they vaguely expected something like the agreeable corruptions of the Midway Plaisance. The idea of her colonial progress with which Germany is trying to affect the home-keeping imagination of her people was illustrated by an encampment of savages from her Central-African possessions. They were getting their supper at the moment the Marches saw them, and were crouching half naked around the fires under the kettles, and shivering from the cold, but they were not very characteristic of the imperial expansion, unless perhaps when an old man in a red blanket suddenly sprang up with a knife in his hand, and began to chase a boy round the camp. The boy was lighter-footed, and easily outran the sage, who tripped at times on his blanket. None of the other Central-Africans seemed to care for the race, and without waiting for the event, the American spectators ordered themselves trundled away to another idle feature of the fair, where they hoped to amuse themselves with the image of Old Leipsic.

This was so faithfully studied from the past in its narrow streets and Gothic houses that it was almost as picturesque as the present epoch in the old streets of Hamburg. A drama had just begun to be represented on a platform of the public square in front of a fourteenth-century beer-house, with people talking from the windows round, and revellers in the costume of the period drinking beer and eating sausages at tables in the open air. Their eating and drinking were real, and in the midst of it a real rain began to pour down upon them, without affecting them any more than if they had been Germans of the nineteenth century. But it drove the Americans to a shelter from which they could not see the play, and when it stopped they made their way back to their hotel.

Their car was full of returning pleasurers, some of whom were happy beyond the sober wont of the fatherland. The conductor took a special interest in his tipsy passengers, trying to keep them in order, and genially entreating them to be quiet when they were too obstreperous. From time to time he got some of them off, and then, when he remounted the car, he appealed to the remaining passengers for their sympathy with an innocent smile, which the Americans, still strange to the unjoyous physiognomy of the German Empire, failed to value at its rare worth.

Before he slept that night March tried to assemble from the experiences and impressions of the day some facts which he would not be ashamed of as a serious observer of life in Leipsic, and he remembered that their guide had said house-rent was very low. He generalized from the guide's content with his fee that the Germans were not very rapacious ; and he became quite irrelevantly aware that in Germany no man's clothes fitted him, or seemed expected to fit him ; that the women dressed somewhat better, and were rather pretty sometimes, and that they had feet as large as the kind hearts of the Germans of every age and sex. He was able to note, rather more freshly, that with all their kindness the Germans were a very nervous people, if not irritable, and at the least cause gave way to an agitation, which indeed quickly passed, but was violent while it lasted. Several times that day he had seen encounters between the *portier* and guests at the hotel which promised violence, but which ended peacefully as soon as some simple question of train-time was solved. The encounters always left the *portier* purple and perspiring, as any agitation must with a man so tight in his livery. He bemoaned himself after one of them as the victim of an unhappy calling, in which he could take no ex-

ercise. "It is a life of excitements, but not
of movements," he explained to March ; and
when he learned where he was going, he re-
gretted that he could not go to Carlsbad too.
" For sugar ?" he asked, as if there were over-
much of it in his own make.

March felt the tribute, but he had to say,
" No ; liver."

" Ah !" said the *portier*, with the air of fail-
ing to get on common ground with him.

XXIV

THE next morning was so fine that it would have been a fine morning in America. Its beauty was scarcely sullied even subjectively by the telegram which the *portier* sent after the Marches from the hotel saying that their missing trunk had not yet been found, and their spirits were as light as the gay little clouds which blew about in the sky, when their train drew out in the sunshine brilliant on the charming landscape all the way to Carlsbad. A fatherly *traeger* had done his best to get them the worst places in a non-smoking compartment, but had succeeded so poorly that they were very comfortable, with no companions but a mother and daughter, who spoke German in soft low tones together. Their compartment was pervaded by tobacco fumes from the smokers, but as these were twice as many as the non-smokers, it was only

237

fair, and after March had got a window open, it did not matter, really.

He asked leave of the strangers in his German, and they consented in theirs; but he could not master the secret of the window-catch, and the elder lady said in English, "Let me show you," and came to his help. The occasion for explaining that they were Americans and accustomed to different car windows was so tempting that Mrs. March could not forbear, and the other ladies were affected as deeply as she could wish. Perhaps they were the more affected because it presently appeared that they had cousins in New York whom she knew of, and that they were acquainted with an American family that had passed a winter in Berlin. Life likes to do these things handsomely, and it easily turned out that this was a family of intimate friendship with the Marches; the names familiarly spoken abolished all strangeness between the travellers; and they entered into a comparison of tastes, opinions, and experiences, from which it seemed that the objects and interests of cultivated people in Berlin were quite the same as those of cultivated people in New York. Each of the parties to the discovery disclaimed any superiority for their respective civilizations; they wished rather to ascribe a greater charm and virtue to the alien conditions; and they acquired such merit with one another that when the German ladies got

out of the train at Franzensbad, the mother offered Mrs. March an ingenious folding foot-stool which she had admired. In fact she left her with it clasped to her breast, and bowing speechless towards the giver in a vain wish to express her gratitude.

"That was very pretty of her, my dear," said March. "*You* couldn't have done that."

"No," she confessed ; "I shouldn't have had the courage. The courage of my emotions," she added, thoughtfully.

"Ah, that's the difference ! A Berliner could do it, and a Bostonian couldn't. Do you think it's so much better to have the courage of your convictions ?"

"I don't know. It seems to me that I'm less and less certain of everything that I used to be sure of."

He laughed, and then he said, "I was think-ing how, on our wedding journey, long ago, that Gray Sister at the Hôtel Dieu in Quebec offered you a rose."

"Well ?"

"That was to your pretty youth. Now the gracious stranger gives you a folding stool."

"To rest my poor old feet. Well, I would rather have it than a rose, now."

"You bent towards her at just the slant you had when you took the flower that time ; I noticed it. I didn't see that you looked so very different. To be sure the roses in your cheeks have turned into rosettes ; but rosettes are very nice, and they're much more permanent ; I prefer them ; they will keep in any climate."

She suffered his mockery with an appreciative sigh. "Yes, our age caricatures our youth, doesn't it ?"

"I don't think it gets much fun out of it," he assented.

"No ; but it can't help it. I used to rebel against it when it first began. I did enjoy being young."

"You did, my dear," he said, taking her hand tenderly ; she withdrew it, because though she could bear his sympathy, her New England nature could not bear its expression. "And so did I ; and we were both young a long time. Travelling brings the past back, don't you think ? There at that restaurant, where we stopped for dinner—"

"Yes, it was charming ! Just as it used to be ! With that white cloth, and those tall shining bottles of wine, and the fruit in the centre, and the dinner in courses, and that young waiter who spoke English and was so nice ! I'm never going home ; *you* may, if you like."

"You bragged to those ladies about our dining-cars ; and you said that our railroad restaurants were quite as good as the European."

"I had to do that. But I knew better; they don't begin to be."

"Perhaps not; but I've been thinking that travel is a good deal alike everywhere. It's the expression of the common civilization of the world. When I came out of that restaurant and ran the train down, and then found that it didn't start for fifteen minutes, I wasn't sure whether I was at home or abroad. And when we changed cars at Eger, and got into this train which had been baking in the sun for us outside the station, I didn't know but I was back in the good old Fitchburg depot. To be sure, Wallenstein wasn't assassinated at Boston, but I forgot his murder at Eger, and so that came to the same thing. It's these confounded fifty odd years. I used to recollect everything."

He had got up and was looking out of the window at the landscape, which had not grown less amiable in growing rather more slovenly since they had crossed the Saxon border into Bohemia. All the morning and early afternoon they had run through lovely levels of harvest, where men were cradling the wheat and women were binding it into sheaves in the narrow fields between black spaces of forest. After they left Eger, there was something more picturesque and less thrifty in the farming among the low hills which they gradually mounted to uplands where they tasted a moun-

243

tain quality in the thin pure air. The railroad stations were shabbier; there was an indefinable touch of something Southern in the scenery and the people. Lilies were rocking on the sluggish reaches of the streams, and where the current quickened, tall wheels were lifting water for the fields in circles of brimming and spilling pockets. Along the embankments where a new track was being laid, barefooted women were at work with pick and spade and barrow, and little yellow-haired girls were lugging large white-headed babies, and watching the train go by. At an up grade where it slowed in the ascent he began to throw out to the children the pfennigs which had been left over from the passage in Germany, and he pleased himself with his bounty, till the question whether the children could spend the money forced itself upon him. He sat down feeling less like a good genius than a cruel magician who had tricked them with false wealth; but he kept his remorse to himself, and tried to interest his wife in the difference of social and civic ideal expressed in the change of the inhibitory placards at the car windows, which in Germany had strongliest forbidden him to outlean himself, and now in Austria entreated him not to outbow himself. She refused to take part in the speculation, or to debate the yet nicer problem involved by the placarded prayer in the wash - room to the

Messrs. Travellers not to take away the soap ;
and suddenly he felt himself as tired as she
looked, with that sense of the futility of travel
which lies in wait for every one who profits by
travel.

XXV

THEY found Burnamy expecting them at
the station in Carlsbad, and she scolded
him like a mother for taking the trouble
to meet them, while she kept back for the present any sign of knowing that he had stayed
over a day with the Triscoes in Leipsic. He
was as affectionately glad to see her and her husband as she could have wished, but she would
have liked it better if he had owned up at once
about Leipsic. He did not, and it seemed to
her that he was holding her at arm's-length in
his answers about his employer. He would not
say how he liked his work, or how he liked Mr.
Stoller ; he merely said that they were at
Pupp's together, and that he had got in a good
day's work already ; and since he would say no
more, she contented herself with that.

The long drive from the station to the hotel
was by streets that wound down the hill-side

like those of an Italian mountain town, between gay stuccoed houses, of Southern rather than of Northern architecture; and the impression of a Latin country was heightened at a turn of the road which brought into view a colossal crucifix, planted against a curtain of dark green foliage, on the brow of one of the wooded heights that surround Carlsbad. When they reached the level of the Tepl, the hill-fed torrent that brawls through the little city under pretty bridges within walls of solid masonry, they found themselves in almost the only vehicle on a brilliant promenade thronged with a cosmopolitan world. Germans in every manner of misfit; Polish Jews in long black gabardines, with tight corkscrew curls on their temples under their black velvet derbys; Austrian officers in tight corsets; Greek priests in flowing robes and brimless high hats; Russians in caftans and Cossacks in Astrakhan caps, accented the more homogeneous masses of western Europeans, in which it would have been hard to say which were English, French, or Italians. Among the vividly dressed ladies, some were imaginably Parisian from their *chic* costumes, but they might easily have been Hungarians or Levantines of taste; some Americans who might have passed unknown in the perfection of their dress gave their nationality away in the flat wooden tones of their voices, which made themselves heard

247

above the low hum of talk and the whisper of the innumerable feet.

The omnibus worked its way at a slow walk among the promenaders going and coming between the rows of pollard locusts on one side and the bright walls of the houses on the other. Under the trees were tables, served by pretty, bareheaded girls who ran to and from the restaurants across the way. On both sides flashed and glittered the little shops full of silver, glass, jewelry, terra-cotta figurines, wood-carvings, and all the idle frippery of watering-place traffic. They suggested Paris, and they suggested Saratoga, and then they were of Carlsbad and of no place else in the world, as the crowd which might have been that of other cities at certain moments could only have been of Carlsbad in its habitual effect.

"Do you like it?" asked Burnamy as if he owned the place, and Mrs. March saw how simple-hearted he was in his reticence, after all. She was ready to bless him when they reached the hotel and found that his interest had got them the only rooms left in the house. This satisfied in her the passion for size which is at the bottom of every American heart, and which perhaps above all else marks us the youngest of the peoples. We pride ourselves on the bigness of our own things, but we are not ungenerous, and when we go to Europe and find things bigger than ours, we are magnanimously happy in them. Pupp's, in its altogether different way, was larger than any hotel at Saratoga or at Niagara; and when Burnamy told her that it sometimes fed fifteen thousand people a day in the height of the season, she was personally proud of it.

She waited with him in the rotunda of the hotel while the secretary led March off to look at the rooms reserved for them, and Burnamy hospitably turned the revolving octagonal case in the centre of the rotunda where the names of the guests were put up. They were of all nations, but there were so many New-Yorkers whose names ended in *berg*, and *thal*, and *stern*, and *baum* that she seemed to be gazing upon a cyclorama of the signs on Broadway. A large man of unmistakable American make, but with so little that was of New England or New York in his presence that she might not at once have thought him American, lounged towards them with a quill toothpick in the corner of his mouth. He had a jealous blue eye, into which he seemed trying to put a friendly light; his straight mouth stretched in a voluntary smile above his tawny chin-beard, and he wore his soft hat so far back from his high forehead (it showed to the crown when he took his hat off) that he had the effect of being uncovered.

At his approach Burnamy turned, and with a flush said: "Oh! Let me introduce Mr. Stoller, Mrs. March."

Stoller took his toothpick out of his mouth and bowed ; then he seemed to remember, and took off his hat. "You see Jews enough here to make you feel at home?" he asked ; and he added : "Well, we got some of 'em in Chicago, too, I guess. This young man"—he twisted his head towards Burnamy—"found you easy enough?"

"It was very good of him to meet us," Mrs. March began. "We didn't expect—"

"Oh, that's all right," said Stoller, putting his toothpick back, and his hat on. "We'd got through for the day ; my doctor won't let me work all I want to, here. Your husband's going to take the cure, they tell me. Well, he wants to go to a good doctor, first. You can't go and drink these waters hit or miss. I found *that* out before I came here."

"Oh no," said Mrs. March, and she wished to explain how they had been advised ; but he said to Burnamy :

"I sha'n't want you again till ten to-morrow morning. Don't let me interrupt you," he added patronizingly to Mrs. March. He put his hand up towards his hat, and sauntered away out of the door.

Burnamy did not speak ; and she only asked at last, to relieve the silence, "Is Mr. Stoller an American?"

"Why, I suppose so," he answered, with an uneasy laugh. "His people were German emi-

"'YOU CAN'T GO AND DRINK THESE WATERS HIT OR MISS'"

grants who settled in southern Indiana. That makes him as much American as any of us, doesn't it?"

Burnamy spoke with his mind on his French-Canadian grandfather, who had come down through Detroit, when their name was Bonami; but Mrs. March answered from her eight generations of New England ancestry, "Oh, for the West, yes, perhaps," and they neither of them said anything more about Stoller.

In their room, where she found March waiting for her amidst their arriving baggage, she was so full of her pent-up opinions of Burnamy's patron that she would scarcely speak of the view from their windows of the wooded hills up and down the Tepl. "Yes, yes; very nice, and I know I shall enjoy it ever so much. But I don't know what you *will* think of that poor young Burnamy!"

"Why, what's happened to him?"

"Happened? *Stoller's* happened."

"Oh, have you seen him already? Well?"

"Well, if you had been going to pick out that type of man, you'd have rejected *him*, because you'd have said he was too pat. He's like an actor made up for a Western million-aire. Do you remember that American in *L'Étrangère* which Bernhardt did in Boston when she first came? He looks exactly like that, and he has the *worst* manners. He stood

253

talking to me with his hat on and a toothpick in his mouth ; and he made me feel as if he had bought *me*, along with Burnamy, and had paid too much. If you don't give him a setting down, Basil, I shall never speak to you ; that's all. I'm sure Burnamy is in some trouble with him ; he's got some sort of hold upon him ; what it *could* be in such a short time, *I* can't imagine ; but if ever a man seemed to be in a man's power, *he* does, in *his !*"

"Now," said March, "your pronouns have got so far beyond me that I think we'd better let it all go till after supper ; perhaps I shall see Stoller myself by that time."

She had been deeply stirred by her encounter with Stoller, but she entered with impartial intensity into the fact that the elevator at Pupp's had the characteristic of always coming up and never going down with passengers. It was locked into its closet with a solid door, and there was no bell to summon it, or any place to take it except on the ground-floor ; but the stairs by which she could descend were abundant and stately ; and on one landing there was the lithograph of one of the largest and ugliest hotels in New York ; how ugly it was she said she should never have known if she had not seen it there.

The dining-room was divided into the grand saloon, where they supped amid rococo sculptures and frescoes, and the glazed veranda opening by vast windows on a spread of tables without, which were already filling up for the evening concert. Around them at the different tables there were groups of faces and figures fascinating in their strangeness, with that distinction which abashes our American level in the presence of European inequality.

"How simple and unimpressive we are, Basil," she said, "beside all these people! I used to feel it in Europe when I was young, and now I'm certain that we must seem like two faded-in old village photographs. We don't even look intellectual! I hope we look *good*."

"I know *I* do," said March. The waiter went for their supper, and they joined in guessing the different nationalities in the room. A French party was easy enough; a Spanish mother and daughter were not difficult, though whether they were not South-American remained uncertain; two elderly maiden ladies were unmistakably of central Massachusetts, and were obviously of a book-club culture that had left no leaf unturned; some Triestines gave themselves away by their Venetian accent; but a large group at a farther table were unassignable in the strange language which they clattered loudly together, with bursts of laughter. They were a family party of old and young, they were having a

255

good time, with a freedom which she called baronial; the ladies wore white satin, or black lace, but the men were in sack-coats; she chose to attribute them, for no reason but their outlandishness, to Transylvania. March pretended to prefer a table full of Germans, who were unmistakably bourgeois, and yet of intellectual effect. He chose as his favorite a middle-aged man of learned aspect, and they both decided to think of him as the Herr Professor, but they did not imagine how perfectly the title fitted him till he drew a long comb from his waistcoat-pocket and combed his hair and beard with it above the table.

The wine wrought with the Transylvanians, and they all jargoned together at once, and laughed at the jokes passing among them. One old gentleman had a peculiar fascination from the infantine innocence of his gums when he threw his head back to laugh, and showed an upper jaw toothless except for two incisors, standing guard over the chasm between. Suddenly he choked, coughed to relieve himself, hawked, held his napkin up before him, and—

"*Noblesse oblige*," said March, with the tone of irony which he reserved for his wife's preoccupations with aristocracies of all sorts. "I think I prefer my Hair Professor, bourgeois as he is."

The ladies attributively of central Massachusetts had risen from their table, and were making for the door without having paid for their supper. The head waiter ran after them; with a real delicacy for their mistake he explained that though in most places meals were charged in the bill, it was the custom in Carlsbad to pay for them at the table; one could see that he was making their error a pleasant adventure to them which they could laugh over together, and write home about without a pang.

"And I," said Mrs. March, shamelessly abandoning the party of the aristocracy, "prefer the manners of the lower classes."

"Oh yes," he admitted. "The only manners we have at home are black ones. But you mustn't lose courage. Perhaps the nobility are not always so baronial."

"I don't know whether we have manners at home," she said, "and I don't believe I care. At least we have decencies."

"Don't be a jingo," said her husband.

XXVI

THOUGH Stoller had formally discharged
Burnamy from duty for the day, he
was not so full of resources in himself
and he had not so general an acquaintance in
the hotel but he was glad to have the young
fellow make up to him in the reading-room that
night. He laid down a New York paper ten
days old in despair of having left any American news in it, and pushed several continental
Anglo-American papers aside with his elbow
as he gave a contemptuous glance at the foreign journals, in Bohemian, Hungarian, German, French, and Italian, which littered the
large table.

"I wonder," he said, "how long it'll take 'em,
over here, to catch on to our way of having
pictures?"

Burnamy had come to his newspaper work
since illustrated journalism was established,

and he had never had any shock from it at home, but so sensitive is youth to environment that after four days in Europe the New York paper Stoller had laid down was already hideous to him. From the politic side of his nature, however, he temporized with Stoller's preference. "I suppose it will be some time yet."

"I wish," said Stoller, with a savage disregard of expressed sequences and relevancies, "I could ha' got some pictures to send home with that letter this afternoon; something to show how they do things here, and be a kind of object-lesson." This term had come up in a recent campaign when some employers, by shutting down their works, were teaching their employees what would happen if the employees voted their political opinions into effect, and Stoller had then mastered its meaning and was fond of using it. "I'd like 'em to see the woods around here that the city owns, and the springs, and the donkey-carts, and the theatre, and everything, and give 'em some practical ideas."

Burnamy made an uneasy movement.

"I'd 'a' liked to put 'em alongside of some of our improvements, and show how a town can be carried on when it's managed on business principles. Why didn't you think of it?"

"Really, I don't know," said Burnamy, with a touch of resentment.

They had not met the evening before on the

best of terms. Stoller had expected Burnamy twenty-four hours earlier, and had shown his displeasure with him for loitering a day at Leipsic which he might have spent at Carlsbad; and Burnamy had been unsatisfactory in accounting for the delay. But he had taken hold so promptly and so intelligently that by working far into the night, and through the whole forenoon, he had got Stoller's crude mass of notes into shape, and had sent off in time for the first steamer the letter which was to appear over the proprietor's name in his paper. It was a sort of rough but very full study of the Carlsbad city government, the methods of taxation, the municipal ownership of the springs and the lands, and the public control in everything. It condemned the aristocratic constitution of the municipality, but it charged heavily in favor of the purity, beneficence, and wisdom of the administration, under which there was no poverty and no idleness, and which was managed like any large business.

Stoller had sulkily recurred to his displeasure, once or twice, and Burnamy had suffered it submissively until now. But now, at the change in Burnamy's tone, he changed his manner a little.

" Seen your friends since supper ?" he asked.

" Only a moment. They are rather tired, and they've gone to bed."

" That the fellow that edits that book you write for ?"

"Yes; he owns it, too."

The notion of any sort of ownership moved Stoller's respect, and he asked, more deferentially, " Makin' a good thing out of it ?"

"A living, I suppose. Some of the high-class weeklies feel the competition of the ten-cent monthlies. But *Every Other Week* is about the best thing we have got in the literary way, and I guess it's holding its own."

" Have to, to let the editor come to Carlsbad," Stoller said, with a return to the sourness of his earlier mood. " I don't know as I care much for his looks ; I seen him when he came in with you. No snap to him." He clicked shut the penknife he had been paring his nails with, and started up with the abruptness which marked all his motions, mental and physical ; as he walked heavily out of the room he said, without looking round at Burnamy, "You want to be ready by half past ten at the latest."

Stoller's father and mother were poor emigrants who made their way to the West with the instinct for a sordid prosperity native to their race and class ; and they set up a small butcher-shop in the little Indiana town where their son was born, and throve in it from the start. He could remember his mother helping his father make the sausage and head-cheese and pickle the pigs' feet which they took turns in selling at as great a price as they could extort from the townspeople. She was a good

261

and tender mother, and when her little Yaw-cup, as the boys called Jacob in mimicry after her, had grown to school-going age, she taught him to fight the Americans, who stoned him when he came out of his gate, and mobbed his home-coming; and mocked and tormented him at play-time till they wore themselves into a kindlier mind towards him through the exhaustion of their invention. No one, so far as the gloomy, stocky, rather dense little boy could make out, ever interfered in his behalf; and he grew up in bitter shame for his German origin, which entailed upon him the hard fate of being Dutch among the Americans. He hated his native speech so much that he cried when he was forced to use it with his father and mother at home; he furiously denied it with the boys who proposed to parley with him in it on such terms as "Nix come arouce in de Dytchman's house." He disused it so thoroughly that after his father took him out of school, when he was old enough to help in the shop, he could not get back to it. He regarded his father's business as part of his national disgrace, and at the cost of leaving his home he broke away from it, and informally apprenticed himself to the village blacksmith and wagon-maker. When it came to his setting up for himself in the business he had chosen, he had no help from his father, who had gone on adding dollar to dollar till he was one of the richest men in the place.

Jacob prospered too ; his old playmates, who had used him so cruelly, had many of them come to like him ; but as a Dutchman they never dreamt of asking him to their houses when they were young people, any more than when they were children. He was long deeply in love with an American girl whom he had never spoken to, and the dream of his life was to marry an American. He ended by marrying the daughter of Pferd the brewer, who had been at an American school in Indianapolis, and had come home as fragilely and nasally American as anybody. She made him a good, sickly, fretful wife, and bore him five children, of whom two survived, with no visible taint of their German origin.

In the mean time Jacob's father had died and left his money to his son, with the understanding that he was to provide for his mother, who would gladly have given every cent to him and been no burden to him, if she could. He took her home, and cared tenderly for her as long as she lived ; and she meekly did her best to abolish herself in a household trying so hard to be American. She could not help her native accent, but she kept silence when her son's wife had company ; and when her eldest grand - daughter began very early to have American callers, she went out of the room ; they would not have noticed her if she had stayed.

Before this Jacob had come forward publicly in proportion to his financial importance in the community. He first commended himself to the Better Element by crushing out a strike in his Buggy Works, which were now the largest business interest of the place ; and he rose on a wave of municipal reform to such a height of favor with the respectable classes that he was elected on a citizens' ticket to the Legislature. In the reaction which followed he was barely defeated for Congress ; and was talked of as a dark horse who might be put up for the governorship some day ; but those who knew him best predicted that he would not get far in politics, where his bull-headed business ways would bring him to ruin sooner or later ; they said, "You can't swing a bolt like you can a strike."

When his mother died, he surprised his old neighbors by going to live in Chicago, though he kept his works in the place where he and they had grown up together. His wife died shortly after, and within four years he lost his three eldest children ; his son, it was said, had begun to go wrong first. But the rumor of his increasing wealth drifted back from Chicago ; he was heard of in different enterprises and speculations ; at last it was said that he had bought a newspaper, and then his boyhood friends decided that Jake was going into politics again.

In the wider horizons and opener atmosphere of the great city he came to understand better that to be an American in all respects was not the best. His mounting sense of importance began to be retroactive in the direction of his ancestral home; he wrote back to the little town near Würzburg which his people had come from, and found that he had relatives still living there, some of whom had become people of substance; and about the time his health gave way from life-long gluttony, and he was ordered to Carls-bad, he had pretty much made up his mind to take his younger daughters and put them in school for a year or two in Würzburg, for a little discipline if not education. He had now left them there, to learn the language, which he had forgotten with such heart-burning and shame, and music, for which they had some taste.

The twins loudly lamented their fate, and they parted from their father with open threats of running away ; and in his heart he did not altogether blame them. He came away from Würzburg raging at the disrespect for his money and his standing in business which had brought him a more galling humiliation there than anything he had suffered in his boyhood at Des Vaches. It intensified him in his dear-bought Americanism to the point of wishing to commit lese-majesty in the teeth of some local dignitaries who had snubbed him, and who

seemed to enjoy putting our eagle to shame in
his person ; there was something like the bird
of his step-country in Stoller's pale eyes and
huge beak.

XXVII

MARCH sat with a company of other
patients in the anteroom of the doctor, and when it came his turn to be
prodded and kneaded, he was ashamed at being told he was not so bad a case as he had
dreaded. The doctor wrote out a careful diet-
ary for him, with a prescription of a certain
number of glasses of water at a certain spring,
and a certain number of baths, and a rule for
the walks he was to take before and after eating ; then the doctor patted him on the shoulder and pushed him caressingly out of his
inner office. It was too late to begin his treatment that day, but he went with his wife to
buy a cup, with a strap for hanging it over his
shoulder, and he put it on so as to be an invalid with the others at once ; he came near
forgetting the small napkin of Turkish towel-
ling which they stuffed into their cups, but

happily the shopman called him back in time to sell it him.

At five the next morning he rose, and on his way to the street exchanged with the servants cleaning the hotel stairs the first of the gloomy *Guten Morgens* which usher in the day at Carlsbad. They seemed to be evoked from the darkest recesses of the soul, but the hopeless tone in which they were uttered is probably expressive only of the general despair of getting through with them before night; and March heard the sorrowful salutations on every hand as he joined the straggling current of invalids which swelled on the way past the silent shops and cafés in the Alte Wiese, till it filled the street, and poured out its thousands on the promenade before the classic colonnade of the Mühlbrunn. On the other bank of the Tepl the Sprudel flings its steaming waters by irregular impulses into the air under a pavilion of iron and glass; but the Mühlbrunn is the source of most resort. There is an instrumental concert somewhere in Carlsbad from early rising till bedtime; and now at the Mühlbrunn there was an orchestra already playing; under the pillared porch, as well as before it, the multitude shuffled up and down draining their cups by slow sips, and then taking each his place in the interminable line moving on to replenish them at the spring.

A picturesque majority of Polish Jews, whom

THE BRIDGE AT THE END OF THE COLONNADE

some vice of their climate is said peculiarly to fit for the healing effects of Carlsbad, most took his eye in their long gabardines of rusty black and their derby hats of plush or velvet, with their corkscrew curls coming down before their ears. They were old and young, they were grizzled and red and black, but they seemed all well-to-do; and what impresses one first and last at Carlsbad is that its waters are mainly for the healing of the rich. After the Polish Jews, the Greek priests of Russian race were the most striking figures. There were types of Latin ecclesiastics, who were striking in their way too ; and the uniforms of certain Austrian officers and soldiers brightened the picture. Here and there a southern face, Italian or Spanish or Levantine, looked passionately out of the mass of dull German visages ; for at Carlsbad the Germans, more than any other gentile nation, are to the fore. Their misfits, their absence of style, imparted the prevalent effect ; though now and then among the women a Hungarian, or Pole, or Parisian, or American, relieved the eye which seeks beauty and grace rather than the domestic virtues. There were certain faces, types of discomfort and disease, which appealed from the beginning to the end. A young Austrian, yellow as gold, and a livid South-American, were of a lasting fascination to March.

What most troubled him, in his scrutiny of

271

the crowd, was the difficulty of assigning people to their respective nations, and he accused his age of having dulled his perceptions ; but perhaps it was from their long disuse in his homogeneous American world. The Americans themselves fused with the European races who were often so hard to make out; his fellow‑citizens would not be identified till their bad voices gave them away; he thought the women's voices the worst.

At the springs, a line of young girls with a steady mechanical action dipped the cups into the steaming source, and passed them impersonally up to their owners. With the patients at the Mühlbrunn it was often a half‑hour before one's turn came, and at all a strict etiquette forbade any attempt to anticipate it. The water was merely warm and flat, and after the first repulsion one could forget it. March formed a childish habit of counting ten between the sips, and of finishing the cup with a gulp which ended it quickly ; he varied his walks between cups by going sometimes to a bridge at the end of the colonnade where a group of Triestines were talking Venetian, and sometimes to the little Park beyond the Kurhaus, where some old women were sweeping up from the close sward the yellow leaves which the trees had untidily dropped overnight. He liked to sit there and look at the city beyond the Tepl, where it climbed the wooded heights in

terraces till it lost its houses in the skirts and folds of the forest. Most mornings it rained, quietly, absent-mindedly, and this, with the chill in the air, deepened a pleasant illusion of Quebec offered by the upper town across the stream; but there were sunny mornings when the mountains shone softly through a lustrous mist, and the air was almost warm.

Once in his walk he found himself the companion of Burnamy's employer, whom he had sometimes noted in the line at the Mühlbrunn, waiting his turn, cup in hand, with a face of sullen impatience. Stoller explained that though you could have the water brought to you at your hotel, he chose to go to the spring for the sake of the air; it was something you had got to live through; before he had that young Burnamy to help him he did not know what to do with his time, but now, every minute he was not eating or sleeping he was working; his cure did not oblige him to walk much. He examined March, with a certain mixture of respect and contempt, upon the nature of the literary life, and how it differed from the life of the journalist. He asked if he thought Burnamy would amount to anything as a literary man; he so far assented to March's faith in him as to say, " He's smart." He told of leaving his daughters in school at Würzburg; and upon the whole he moved March with a sense of his pathetic loneliness without moving his

275

liking, as he passed lumberingly on, dangling his cup.

March gave his own cup to the little maid at his spring, and while she gave it to a second, who dipped it and handed it to a third for its return to him, he heard an unmistakable fellow-countryman saying good-morning to them all in English. "Are you going to teach them United States?" he asked of a face with which he knew such an appeal could not fail.

"Well," the man admitted, "I try to teach them *that* much. *They* like it. You are an American? I am glad of it. I have 'most lost the use of my lungs here. I'm a great talker, and I talk to my wife till she's about dead; then I'm out of it for the rest of the day; I can't speak German."

His manner was the free, friendly manner of the West. He must be that sort of un-travelled American whom March had so seldom met, but he was afraid to ask him if this was his first time at Carlsbad lest it should prove the third or fourth. "Are you taking the cure?" he asked instead.

"Oh no. My wife is. She'll be along directly; I come down here and drink the waters to encourage her; doctor said to. That gets me in for the diet, too. I've e't more cooked fruit since I been here than I ever did in *my* life before. Prunes? My Lord, I'm *full* o' prunes! Well, it does me good to see an

SPRUDEL SPRING

American, to know him. I couldn't 'a' told you, if you hadn't have spoken."

"Well," said March, "I shouldn't have been sure of you, either, by your looks."

"Yes, we can't always tell ourselves from these Dutch. But *they* know us, and they don't want us, except just for one thing, and that's our money. I tell *you*, the *Americans* are the chumps over here. Soon's they got all our money, or think they have, they say, 'Here, you Americans, this is my country; you get off'; and we got to get. Ever been over before?"

"A great while ago; so long that I can hardly believe it."

"It's my first time. My name's Otterson; I'm from out in Iowa."

March gave him his name, and added that he was from New York.

"Yes. I thought you was Eastern. But that wasn't an Eastern man you was just with?"

"No; he's from Chicago. He's a Mr. Stoller."

"Not the *buggy* man?"

"I believe he makes buggies."

"Well, you *do* meet everybody here." The Iowan was silent for a moment, as if hushed by the weighty thought. "I wish my wife could have seen him. I just want her to see the man that made our buggy. *I* don't know what's keeping her, this morning," he added, apologetically. " Look at that fellow, will you, tryin' to get away from those women !" A young officer was doing his best to take leave of two ladies, who seemed to be mother and daughter ; they detained him by their united arts, and clung to him with caressing words and looks. He was red in the face with his polite struggles when he broke from them at last. " How they do hang on to a man over here !" the Iowa man continued. "And the Americans are as bad as any. Why, there's one ratty little Englishman up at our place, and our girls just swarm after him ; their mothers are worse. Well, it's so, Jenny," he said to the lady who had joined them, and whom March turned round to see when he spoke to her. "If I wanted a foreigner, I should go in for a *man*. And these officers ! Put their *mus*-taches up at night in curl-papers, they tell *me*. Introduce you to Mrs. Otterson, Mr. March. Well, had your first glass, yet, Jenny ? I'm just going for my second tumbler."

He took his wife back to the spring, and began to tell her about Stoller ; she made no sign of caring for him ; and March felt inculpated. She relented a little towards him as they drank together ; when he said he must be going to breakfast with his wife, she asked where he breakfasted, and said, " Why, *we* go to the Posthof, too." He answered that then they should be sure some time to meet there ; he did not venture further ; he reflected that Mrs. March had her reluctances too ; she distrusted people who had amused or interested him before she met them.

XXVIII

BURNAMY had found the Posthof for them, as he had found most of the other agreeable things in Carlsbad, which he brought to their knowledge one by one, with such forethought that March said he hoped he should be cared for in his declining years as an editor rather than as a father; there was no tenderness like a young contributor's.

Many people from the hotels on the hill found at Pupp's just the time and space between their last cup of water and their first cup of the coffee which was prescribed at Carlsbad; but the Marches were aware somehow from the beginning that Pupp's had not the hold upon the world at breakfast which it had at the mid-day dinner, or at supper on the evenings when the concert was there. Still it was amusing, and they were patient of Burnamy's delay till he could get a morning off from Stoller and go with them to the Posthof. He met Mrs. March in the reading-room, where March was to join them on his way from the springs with his bag of bread. The earlier usage of buying the delicate pink slices of Westphalia ham, which form the chief motive of a Carlsbad breakfast, at a certain shop in the town, and carrying them to the café with you, is no longer of such binding force as the custom of getting your bread at the Swiss bakery. You choose it yourself at the counter, which begins to be crowded by half past seven, and when you have collected the prescribed loaves into the basket of metallic filigree given you by one of the baker's maids, she puts it into a tissue-paper bag of a gay red color, and you join the other invalids streaming away from the bakery, their paper bags making a festive rustling as they go.

Two roads lead out of the town into the lovely meadow-lands, a good mile up the brawling Tepl, before they join on the right side of the torrent, where the Posthof lurks nestled under trees whose boughs let the sun and rain impartially through upon its army of little tables. By this time the slow omnibus plying between Carlsbad and some villages in the valley beyond has crossed from the left bank to the right, and keeps on past half a dozen cafés, where patients whose prescriptions marshal

283

them beyond the Posthof drop off by the dozens and scores.

The road on the left bank of the Tepl is wild and overhung at points with wooded steeps, when it leaves the town ; but on the right it is bordered with shops and restaurants a good part of its length. In leafy nooks between these, uphill walks begin their climb of the mountains, from the foot of votive shrines set round with tablets commemorating in German, French, Russian, Hebrew, Magyar, and Czech, the cure of highwellborns of all those races and languages. Booths glittering with the lapidary's work in the cheaper gems, or full of the ingenious figures of the toy-makers, alternate with the shrines and the cafés on the way to the Posthof, and with their shoulders against the overhanging cliff, spread for the passing crowd a lure of Viennese jewelry in garnets, opals, amethysts, and the like, and of such Bohemian playthings as carrot-eating rabbits, worsted-working cats, dancing-bears, and peacocks that strut about the feet of the passers and expand their iridescent tails in mimic pride.

Burnamy got his charges with difficulty by the shrines in which they felt the far-reflected charm of the crucifixes of the white-hot Italian highways of their early travel, and by the toyshops where they had a mechanical, out-dated impulse to get something for the children, ending in a pang for the fact that they were children no longer. He waited politely while Mrs. March made up her mind that she would not buy any laces of the motherly old women who showed them under pent-roofs on way-side tables; and he waited patiently at the gate of the flower-gardens beyond the shops where March bought lavishly of sweet-pease from the businesslike flower-women, and feigned a grateful joy in them because they knew no English, and gave him a chance of speaking his German.

"You'll find," he said, as they crossed the road again, "that it's well to trifle a good deal; it makes the time pass. I should still be lagging along in my thirties if it hadn't been for fooling, and here I am well on in my fifties, and Mrs. March is younger than ever."

They were at the gate of the garden and grounds of the café at last, and a turn of the path brought them to the prospect of its tables, under the trees, between the two long glazed galleries where the breakfasters take refuge at other tables when it rains; it rains nearly always, and the trunks of the trees are as green with damp as if painted; but that morning the sun was shining. At the verge of the open space a band of pretty serving-maids, each with her name on a silver band pinned upon her breast, met them and bade them a Guten Morgen of almost cheerful note, but gave way to an eager little smiling blonde, who came pushing

285

down the path at sight of Burnamy, and claimed him for her own.

"Ah, Lili! We want an extra good table, this morning. These are some American Excellencies, and you must do your best for them."

"Oh yes," the girl answered in English, after a radiant salutation of the Marches; "I get you one. You are a little more formerly, to-day, and I didn't had one already."

She ran among the tables along the edge of the western gallery, and was far beyond hearing his protest that he was not earlier than usual when she beckoned him to the table she had found. She had crowded it in between two belonging to other girls, and by the time her breakfasters came up she was ready for their order, with the pouting pretence that the girls always tried to rob her of the best places. Burnamy explained proudly when she went that none of the other girls ever got an advantage of her ; she had more custom than any three of them, and she had hired a man to help her carry her orders. The girls were all from the neighboring villages, he said, and they lived at home in the winter on their summer tips ; their wages were nothing, or less, for sometimes they paid for their places.

"What a mass of information !" said March. "How did you come by it ?"

"Newspaper habit of interviewing the universe."

"It's not a bad habit, if one doesn't carry it too far. How did Lili learn her English?"

"She takes lessons in the winter. She's a perfect little electric motor. I don't believe any Yankee girl could equal her."

"She would expect to marry a millionaire if she did. What astonishes one over here is to see how contentedly people prosper along on their own level. And the women do twice the work of the men without expecting to equal them in any other way. At Pupp's, if we go to one end of the out-door restaurant, it takes three men to wait on us: one to bring our coffee or tea, another to bring our bread and meat, and another to make out our bill, and I have to tip all three of them. If we go to the other end, one girl serves us, and I have to give only one fee; I make it less than the least I give any three of the men waiters."

"You ought to be ashamed of that," said his wife.

"I'm not. I'm simply proud of your sex, my dear."

"Women do nearly everything, here," said Burnamy, impartially. "They built that big new Kaiserbad building: mixed the mortar, carried the hods, and laid the stone."

"That makes me prouder of the sex than ever. But come, Mr. Burnamy! Isn't there anybody of polite interest that you know of in this crowd?"

T   289

"Well, I can't say," Burnamy hesitated.

The breakfasters had been thronging into the grove and the galleries; the tables were already filled, and men were bringing other tables in on their heads, and making places for them, with entreaties for pardon everywhere; the proprietor was anxiously directing them; the pretty serving-girls were running to and from the kitchen in a building apart with shrill, sweet promises of haste. The morning sun fell broken through the leaves on the gay hats and dresses of the ladies, and dappled the figures of the men with harlequin patches of light and shade. A tall woman, with a sort of sharpened beauty, and an artificial permanency of tint in her cheeks and yellow hair, came trailing herself up the sun-shot path, and found, with hardy insistence upon the publicity, places for the surly looking, down-faced young man behind her, and for her maid and her black poodle; the dog was like the black poodle out of *Faust*. Burnamy had heard her history; in fact he had already roughed out a poem on it, which he called Europa, not after the old fable, but because it seemed to him that she expressed Europe, on one side of its civilization, and had an authorized place in its order, as she would not have had in ours. She was where she was by a toleration of certain social facts which corresponds in Europe to our reverence for the vested interests. In her history there had been officers and bankers ; even foreign dignitaries ; now there was this sullen young fellow. . . . Burnamy had wondered if it would do to offer his poem to March, but the presence of the original abashed him, and in his mind he had torn the poem up, with a heartache for its aptness.

"I don't believe," he said, "that I recognize any celebrities here."

"I'm sorry," said March. "Mrs. March would have been glad of some Hoheits, some Grafs and Gräfins, or a few Excellenzes, or even some mere wellborns. But we must try to get along with the picturesqueness."

"I'm satisfied with the picturesqueness," said his wife. "Don't worry about me, Mr. Burnamy. *Why* can't we have this sort of thing at home?"

"We're getting something like it in the roof-gardens," said March. "We couldn't have it naturally because the climate is against it, with us. At this time in the morning over there, the sun would be burning the life out of the air, and the flies would be swarming on every table. At nine P.M. the mosquitoes would be eating us up in such a grove as this. So we have to use artifice, and lift our Posthofs above the fly-line and the mosquito-line into the night air. I haven't seen a fly since I came to Europe. I really miss them ; it makes me homesick."

"There are plenty in Italy," his wife suggested.

"We must get down there and get some before we go home. But why did nobody ever tell us that there were no flies in Germany? Why did no traveller ever put it in his book? When your stewardess said so on the steamer, I remember that you regarded it as a bluff." He turned to Burnamy, who was listening with the deference of a contributor: "Isn't Lili rather long? I mean for such a *very* prompt person. Oh no!"

But Burnamy got to his feet, and shouted "Fräulein!" to Lili; with her hireling at her heels she was flying down a distant aisle between the tables, bearing laden trays. She called back, with a face laughing over her shoulder, "In a minute!" and vanished in the crowd.

"Does that mean anything in particular? There's really no hurry."

"Oh, I think she'll come now," said Burnamy. March protested that he had only been amused at Lili's delay; but his wife scolded him for his impatience; she begged Burnamy's pardon, and repeated civilities passed between them. She asked if he did not think some of the young ladies were pretty beyond the European average; a very few had style; the mothers were mostly fat, and not stylish; it was well not to regard the fathers too closely; several old gentlemen were clearing their throats behind their newspapers, with noises that made her quail. There was no one so effective as the Austrian officers, who put themselves a good deal on show, bowing from their hips to favored groups ; with the sun glinting from their eye-glasses, and their hands pressing their sword-hilts, they moved between the tables with the gait of tight-laced women.

"They all wear corsets," Burnamy explained.

"How much you know already !" said Mrs. March. "I can see that Europe won't be lost on you in anything. Oh, who's *that ?*" A lady whose costume expressed Paris at every point glided up the middle aisle of the grove with a graceful tilt. Burnamy was silent. "She must be an American. Do you know who she is?"

"Yes." He hesitated a little to name a woman whose tragedy had once filled the news-papers.

Mrs. March gazed after her with the fasci-nation which such tragedies inspire. "What grace ! Is she beautiful?"

"Very."

Burnamy had not obtruded his knowledge, but somehow Mrs. March did not like his know-ing who she was, and how beautiful. She asked March to look, but he refused.

"Those things are too squalid," he said, and she liked him for saying it ; she hoped it would not be lost upon Burnamy.

One of the waitresses tripped on the steps near them and flung the burden off her tray on the stone floor before her; some of the dishes broke, and the breakfast was lost. Tears came into the girl's eyes and rolled down her hot cheeks. "There! That is what I call tragedy," said March. "She'll have to pay for those things."

"Oh, give her the money, dearest!"

"How can I?"

The girl had just got away with the ruin when Lili and her hireling behind her came bearing down upon them with their three substantial breakfasts on two well-laden trays. She forestalled Burnamy's reproaches for her delay, laughing and bridling, while she set down the dishes of ham and tongue and egg, and the little pots of coffee and frothed milk.

"I could not so soon I wanted, because I was to serve an American princess."

Mrs. March started with proud conjecture of one of those noble international marriages which fill our women with vainglory for such of their compatriots as make them.

"Oh, come now, Lili!" said Burnamy. "We have queens in America, but nothing so low as princesses. This was a queen, wasn't it?"

She referred the case to her hireling, who confirmed her. "All people say it is princess," she insisted.

"Well, if she's a princess we must look her up after breakfast," said Burnamy. "Where is she sitting?"

She pointed at a corner so far off on the other side that no one could be distinguished, and then was gone, with a smile flashed over her shoulder, and her hireling trying to keep up with her.

"We're all very proud of Lili's having a hired man," said Burnamy. "We think it reflects credit on her customers."

March had begun his breakfast with the voracious appetite of an early-rising invalid. "*What* coffee!" He drew a long sigh after the first draught.

"It's said to be made of burnt figs," said Burnamy, from the inexhaustible advantage of his few days' priority in Carlsbad.

"Then let's have burnt figs introduced at home as soon as possible. But why burnt figs? That seems one of those doubts which are more difficult than faith."

"It's not only burnt figs," said Burnamy, with amiable superiority, "if it *is* burnt figs, but it's made after a formula invented by a consensus of physicians, and enforced by the municipality. Every café in Carlsbad makes the same kind of coffee and charges the same price."

"You are leaving us very little to find out for ourselves," sighed March.

"Oh, I know a lot more things. Are you fond of fishing?"

"Not very."

"You can get a permit to catch trout in the Tepl, but they send an official with you who keeps count, and when you have had your sport, the trout belong to the municipality just as they did before you caught them."

"I don't see why that isn't a good notion : the last thing I should want to do would be to eat a fish that I had caught, and that I was personally acquainted with. Well, I'm never going away from Carlsbad. I don't wonder the Germans get themselves out of order if it brings them here."

Burnamy told them a number of facts he said Stoller had got together about the place, and had given him to put in shape. It was run in the interest of people who had got out of order, so that they would keep coming to get themselves in order again ; you could hardly buy an unwholesome meal in the town ; all the cooking was *kurgemäss*. He won such favor with his facts that he could not stop in time ; he said to March, " But if you ever *should* have a fancy for a fish of your personal acquaintance, there's a restaurant up the Tepl, here, where they let you pick out your trout in the water ; then they catch him and broil him for you, and you know what you are eating."

"Is it a municipal restaurant ?"

"Semi-municipal," said Burnamy, laughing.

"We'll take Mrs. March," said her husband, and in her gravity Burnamy felt the limitations

of a woman's sense of humor, which always de-
fine themselves for men so unexpectedly.

He did what he could to get back into her
good graces by telling her what he knew about
distinctions and dignities that he now saw
among the breakfasters. The crowd had grown
denser till the tables were set together in such
labyrinths that any one who left the central
aisle was lost in them. The serving-girls ran
more swiftly to and fro, responding with a more
nervous shrillness to the calls of " Fräulein !
Fräulein !" that followed them. The proprietor, in his bare head, stood like one paralyzed
by his prosperity, which sent up all round him
the clash of knives and crockery, and the con-
fusion of tongues. It was more than an hour
before Burnamy caught Lili's eye, and three
times she promised to come and be paid before
she came. Then she said, " It is so nice, when
you stay a little," and when he told her of the
poor Fräulein who had broken the dishes in her
fall near them, she almost wept with tenderness ; she almost winked with wickedness when
he asked if the American princess was still in
her place.

" Do go and see who it can be !" Mrs. March
entreated. " We'll wait here," and he obeyed.
" I am not sure that I like him," she said, as
soon as he was out of hearing. " I don't know
but he's coarse, after all. It was *very* coarse,
his telling about that fish-restaurant ; and do

297

you approve of his knowing so many people's *taches* already?"

"Would it be any better later?" he asked in turn, leaving the more dangerous question of the fish-restaurant. "He seemed to find you interested."

"It's very different with us; we're not young," she urged, only half seriously.

Her husband laughed. "I see you want me to defend him. Oh, hello!" he cried, and she saw Burnamy coming toward them with a young lady, who was nodding to them from as far as she could see them. "This is the easy kind of thing that would make you blush for the author if you found it in a novel."

XXIX

MRS. MARCH fairly took Miss Triscoe in her arms to kiss her. " Do you know I felt it must be you, all the time ! When did you come ? Where is your father ? What hotel are you staying at ?"

It appeared, while Miss Triscoe was shaking hands with March, that it was last night, and her father was finishing his breakfast, and it was one of the hotels on the hill. On the way back to her father it appeared that he wished to consult March's doctor ; not that there was anything the matter.

The general himself was not much softened by the reunion with his fellow - Americans ; he confided to them that his coffee was poison- ous ; but he seemed, standing up with the Paris- New York *Chronicle* folded in his hand, to have drunk it all. Was March going off on his fore- noon tramp ? He believed that was part of the treatment, which was probably all humbug, though he thought of trying it, now he was there. He was told the walks were fine; he looked at Burnamy as if he had been praising them, and Burnamy said he had been wondering if March would not like to try a mountain path back to his hotel; he said, not so sincerely, that he thought Mrs. March would like it.

"I shall like your account of it," she answered. "But I'll walk back on a level, if you please."

"Oh yes," Miss Triscoe pleaded, "come with us!" She played a little comedy of meaning to go back with her father so gracefully that Mrs. March herself could scarcely have told just where the girl's real purpose of going with Burnamy began to be evident, or just how she managed to make General Triscoe beg to have the pleasure of seeing Mrs. March back to her hotel.

March went with the young people across the meadow behind the Posthof and up into the forest, which began at the base of the mountain. At first they tried to keep him in the range of their talk; but he fell behind more and more, and as the talk narrowed to themselves it was less and less possible to include him in it. When it began to concern their common appreciation of the Marches, they even tried to get out of his hearing.

"They're so young in their thoughts," said

Burnamy, "and they seem as much interested in everything as they could have been thirty years ago. They belong to a time when the world was a good deal fresher than it is now ; don't you think? I mean, in the eighteen-sixties."

"Oh yes, I can see that."

"I don't know why we shouldn't be born older in each generation than people were in the last. Perhaps we are," he suggested.

"I don't know how you mean," said the girl, keeping vigorously up with him ; she let him take the jacket she threw off, but she would not have his hand at the little steeps where he wanted to give it.

"I don't believe I can quite make it out myself. But fancy a man that began to act at twenty, quite unconsciously of course, from the past experience of the whole race—"

"He would be rather a dreadful person, wouldn't he?"

"Rather monstrous, yes," he owned, with a laugh. "But that's where the psychological interest would come in."

As if she did not feel the notion quite pleasant she turned from it. "I suppose you've been writing all sorts of things since you came here."

"Well, it hasn't been such a great while as it's seemed, and I've had Mr. Stoller's psychological interests to look after."

"Oh yes! Do you like him?"

"I don't know. He's a lump of honest sel-
fishness. He isn't bad. You know where to
have him. *He's* simple, too."

"You mean, like Mr. March?"

"I didn't mean that; but why not? They're
not of the same generation, but Stoller isn't
modern."

"I'm very curious to see him," said the girl.

"Do you want me to introduce him?"

"You can introduce him to papa."

They stopped and looked across the curve
of the mountain path, down at March, who
had sunk on a way-side seat, and was mopping
his forehead. He saw them, and called up:
"Don't wait for me. I'll join you, gradually."

"I don't want to lose you," Burnamy called
back, but he kept on with Miss Triscoe. "I
want to get in the Hirschensprung," he explained. "It's the cliff where a hunted deer
leaped down several hundred feet to get away
from an emperor who was after him."

"Oh yes. They have them everywhere."

"Do they? Well, anyway, there's a noble
view up there."

There was no view on the way up. The
Germans' notion of a woodland is everywhere
that of a dense forest such as their barbarous
tribes primevally herded in. It means the
close-set stems of trees, with their tops inter-
woven in a roof of boughs and leaves so dense-

THE HIRSCHENSPRUNG

ly that you may walk dry through it almost as long as a German shower lasts. When the sun shines there is a pleasant greenish light in the aisles, shot here and there with the gold that trickles through. There is nothing of the accident of an American wood in these forests, which have been watched and weeded by man ever since they burst the soil. They remain nurseries, but they have the charm which no human care can alienate. The smell of their bark and their leaves, and of the moist flowerless earth about their roots, came to March where he sat rich with the memories of his country-bred youth, and drugged all consciousness of his long life in cities since, and made him a part of nature, with dulled interests and dimmed perspectives, so that for the moment he had the enjoyment of an absolute present. There was no wild life to penetrate his isolation ; no birds, not a squirrel, not an insect ; an old man who had bidden him good-morning, as he came up, kept fumbling at the path with his hoe, and was less intrusive than if he had not been there.

March thought of the impassioned existence of these young people playing the inevitable comedy of hide and seek which the youth of the race has played from the beginning of time. The other invalids who haunted the forest, and passed up and down before him in fulfilment of their several prescriptions, had a thin unreality in spite of the physical bulk that prevailed among them, and they heightened the relief that the forest-spirit brought him from the strenuous contact of that young drama. He had been almost painfully aware that the persons in it had met, however little they knew it, with an eagerness intensified by their brief separation, and he fancied it was the girl who had unconsciously operated their reunion in response to the young man's longing, her will making itself electrically felt through space by that sort of wireless telegraphy which love has long employed, and science has just begun to imagine.

He would have been willing that they should get home alone, but he knew that his wife would require an account of them from him, and though he could have invented something of the kind, if it came to the worst, he was aware that it would not do for him to arrive without them. The thought goaded him from his seat, and he joined the upward procession of his fellow-sick, as it met another procession straggling downward ; the ways branched in all directions, with people on them everywhere, bent upon building up in a month the health which they would spend the rest of the year in demolishing.

He came upon his charges unexpectedly at a turn of the path, and Miss Triscoe told him that he ought to have been with them for the view from the Hirschensprung. It was mag-

nificent, she said, and she made Burnamy cor-
roborate her praise of it, and agree with her
that it was worth the climb a thousand times ;
he modestly accepted the credit she appeared
willing to give him, of inventing the Hirschensprung.

XXX

BETWEEN his work for Stoller and what
sometimes seemed the obstructiveness
of General Triscoe, Burnamy was not
very much with Miss Triscoe. He was not de-
vout, but he went every Sunday to the pretty
English church on the hill, where he contributed beyond his means to the support of the
English clergy on the Continent, for the sake
of looking at her back hair during the service,
and losing himself in the graceful lines which
defined the girl's figure from the slant of her
flowery hat to the point where the pew-top
crossed her elastic waist. One happy morning
the general did not come to church, and he had
the fortune to walk home with her to her pension, where she lingered with him a moment,
and almost made him believe she might be
going to ask him to come in.

The next evening, when he was sauntering

THE ENGLISH CHURCH

down the row of glittering shops beside the Tepl, with Mrs. March, they overtook the general and his daughter at a place where the girl was admiring some stork-scissors in the window; she said she wished she were still little, so that she could get them. They walked home with the Triscoes, and then he hurried Mrs. March back to the shop. The man had already put up his shutters, and was just closing his door, but Burnamy pushed in, and asked to look at the stork-scissors they had seen in the window. The gas was out, and the shopman lighted a very dim candle, to show them.

"I knew you wanted to get them for her, after what she said, Mrs. March," he laughed nervously, "and you must let me lend you the money."

"Why, of course!" she answered, joyfully humoring his feint. "Shall I put my card in for the man to send home to her with them?"

"Well—no. No. Not *your* card—exactly. Or, yes! Yes, you must, I suppose."

They made the hushing street gay with their laughter; the next evening Miss Triscoe came upon the Marches and Burnamy where they sat after supper listening to the concert at Pupp's, and thanked Mrs. March for the scissors. Then she and Burnamy had their laugh again, and Miss Triscoe joined them, to her father's frowning mystification. He stared round for a table; they were all taken, and he could not refuse the interest Burnamy made with the waiters to bring them one and crowd it in. He had to ask him to sup with them, and Burnamy sat down and heard the concert through beside Miss Triscoe.

"What is so tremendously amusing in a pair of stork-scissors?" March demanded, when his wife and he were alone.

"Why, I was wanting to tell you, dearest," she began, in a tone which he felt to be wheedling, and she told the story of the scissors.

"Look here, my dear! Didn't you promise to let this love-affair alone?"

"That was on the ship. And besides, what would *you* have done, I should like to know? Would you have refused to let him buy them for her?" She added, carelessly: "He wants us to go to the Kurhaus ball with him."

"Oh, *does* he!"

"Yes. He says he knows that she can get her father to let her go if we will chaperon them. And I promised that you would."

"That *I* would?"

"It will do just as well if you go. And it will be very amusing; you can see something of Carlsbad society."

"But I'm not going!" he declared. "It would interfere with my cure. The sitting up late would be bad enough, but I should get very hungry, and I should eat potato salad and

sausages, and drink beer, and do all sorts of unwholesome things."

"Nonsense! The refreshments will be *kurgemäss*, of course."

"You can go yourself," he said.

A ball is not the same thing for a woman
after fifty as it is before twenty, but still it has
claims upon the imagination, and the novel
circumstance of a ball in the Kurhaus in Carlsbad enhanced these for Mrs. March. It was
the annual reunion which is given by municipal authority in the large hall above the
bath-rooms; it is frequented with safety and
pleasure by curious strangers, and now, upon
reflection, it began to have for Mrs. March the
charm of duty; she believed that she could
finally have made March go in her place, but
she felt that she ought really to go in his, and
save him from the late hours and the late
supper.

"Very well, then," she said, at last, "I *will*
go."

It appeared that any civil person might go
to the reunion who chose to pay two florins
and a half. There must have been some sort
of restriction, and the ladies of Burnamy's
party went with a good deal of amused curiosity to see what the distinctions were; but
they saw none unless it was in the advantages
which the military had. The long hall over
the bath-rooms shaped itself into a space for

the dancing at one end, and all the rest of it was filled with tables, which at half past eight were crowded with people, eating, drinking, and smoking. The military enjoyed the monopoly of a table next the rail dividing the dancing from the dining space. There the tight-laced Herr Hauptmanns and Herr Lieutenants sat at their sausage and beer and cigars in the intervals of the waltzes, and strengthened themselves for a foray among the gracious Fraus and Fräuleins on the benches lining three sides of the dancing space. From the gallery above many civilian spectators looked down upon the gayety, and the dress-coats of a few citizens figured among the uniforms.

As the evening wore on some ladies of greater fashion found their way to the dancing-floor, and towards ten o'clock it became rather crowded. A party of American girls showed their Paris dresses in the transatlantic versions of the waltz. At first they danced with the young men who came with them ; but after a while they yielded to the custom of the place, and danced with any of the officers who asked them.

"I know it's the custom," said Mrs. March to Miss Triscoe, who was at her side in one of the waltzes she had decided to sit out, so as not to be dancing all the time with Burnamy, "but I never can like it without an introduction."

" No," said the girl, with the air of putting temptation decidedly away, " I don't believe papa would, either."

A young officer came up, and drooped in mute supplication before her. She glanced at Mrs. March, who turned her face away; and she excused herself with the pretence that she had promised the dance, and by good fortune, Burnamy, who had been unscrupulously waltzing with a lady he did not know, came up at the moment. She rose and put her hand on his arm, and they both bowed to the officer before they whirled away. The officer looked after them with amiable admiration; then he turned to Mrs. March with a light of banter in his friendly eyes, and was unmistakably asking her to dance. She liked his ironical daring, she liked it so much that she forgot her objection to partners without introductions; she forgot her fifty-odd years; she forgot that she was a mother of grown children and even a mother-in-law; she remembered only the step of her out-dated waltz. It seemed to be modern enough for the cheerful young officer, and they were suddenly revolving with the rest. A tide of long-forgotten girlhood welled up in her heart, and she laughed as she floated off on it past the astonished eyes of Miss Triscoe and Burnamy. She saw them falter, as if they had lost their step in their astonishment; then they seemed both to vanish, and her partner had released her, and was helping Miss Triscoe up from the floor; Burnamy was brushing the dust from his knees, and the citizen who had bowled them over was boisterously apologizing and incessantly bowing.

"Oh, are you hurt?" Mrs. March implored. "I'm sure you must be killed; and I did it! I don't know what I was thinking of!"

The girl laughed. "I'm not hurt a bit!"

They had one impulse to escape from the place, and from the sympathy and congratulation. In the dressing-room she declared again that she was all right. "How beautifully you waltz, Mrs. March!" she said, and she laughed again, and would not agree with her that she had been ridiculous. "But I'm glad those American girls didn't see me. And I can't be too thankful papa didn't come!"

Mrs. March's heart sank at the thought of what General Triscoe would think of her when he knew everything. "You must tell him I did it. I can never lift up my head!"

"No, I shall not. No one did it," said the girl, magnanimously. She looked down sidelong at her draperies. "I *was* so afraid I had torn my dress! I certainly heard something rip."

It was one of the skirts of Burnamy's coat, which he had caught into his hand and held in place till he could escape to the men's dressing-room, where he had it pinned up so skilfully that the damage was not suspected by the ladies. He had banged his knee abominably too ; but they did not suspect that either, as he limped home on the air beside them, first to Miss Triscoe's pension, and then to Mrs. March's hotel.

It was quite eleven o'clock, which at Carlsbad is as late as three in the morning anywhere else, when she let herself into her room. She decided not to tell her husband, then ; and even at breakfast, which they had at the Posthof, she had not got to her confession, though she had told him everything else about the ball, when the young officer with whom she had danced passed between the tables near her. He caught her eye and bowed with a smile of so much meaning that March asked, " Who's your pretty young friend ?"

" Oh, *that !* " she answered, carelessly. "That was one of the officers at the ball," and she laughed.

" You seem to be in the joke too," he said. " What is it ?"

" Oh, something. I'll tell you some time. Or perhaps you'll find out."

" I'm afraid you won't let me wait."

" No, I won't," and now she told him. She had expected teasing, ridicule, sarcasm, anything but the psychological interest mixed with a sort of retrospective tenderness which he showed. " I wish I could have seen you ; I always thought you danced well." He added : " It seems that you need a chaperon too."

The next morning, after March and General Triscoe had started off upon one of their hill climbs, the young people made her go with them for a walk up the Tepl, as far as the café of the Freundschaftsaal. In the grounds an artist in silhouettes was cutting out the likenesses of people who supposed themselves to have profiles, and they begged Mrs. March to sit for hers. It was so good that she insisted on Miss Triscoe's sitting in turn, and then Burnamy. Then he had the inspiration to propose that they should all three sit together, and it appeared that such a group was within the scope of the silhouettist's art ; he posed them in his little bower, and while he was mounting the picture they took turns, at five kreutzers each, in listening to American tunes played by his Edison phonograph.

Mrs. March felt that all this was weakening her moral fibre ; but she tried to draw the line at letting Burnamy keep the group. " Why not ?" he pleaded.

"You oughtn't to ask," she returned. " You've no business to have Miss Triscoe's picture, if you must know."

" But you're there to chaperon us," he persisted.

He began to laugh, and they all laughed when she said, " In a silhouette you need a chaperon who doesn't lose her head." But it seemed useless to hold out after that, and she heard herself asking, "Shall we let him keep it, Miss Triscoe?"

Burnamy went off to his work with Stoller, carrying the silhouette with him, and she kept on with Miss Triscoe to her hotel. In turning from the gate after she parted with the girl she found herself confronted with Mrs. Adding and Rose. The ladies exclaimed at each other in an astonishment from which they had to recover before they could begin to talk, but from the first moment Mrs. March perceived that Mrs. Adding had something to say. The more freely to say it she asked Mrs. March into her hotel, which was in the same street with the pension of the Triscoes, and she let her boy go off about the exploration of Carlsbad ; he promised to be back in an hour.

"Well, *now* what scrape are you in ?" March asked, when his wife came home, and began to put off her things, with signs of excitement which he could not fail to note. He was lying down after a long tramp, and he seemed very comfortable.

His question suggested something of anterior import, and she told him about the silhouettes, and the advantage the young people had taken of their power over her through their knowledge of her foolish behavior at the ball.

319

He said, lazily : "They seem to be working you for all you're worth. Is that it ?"

"No ; there is something worse. Something's happened which throws all of that *quite* in the shade. Mrs. Adding is here."

"Mrs. Adding ?" repeated March, with a dimness for names which his wife would not allow was growing on him.

"Don't be stupid, dear ! Mrs. Adding, who sat opposite Mr. Kenby on the *Norumbia*. The mother of the nice boy."

"Oh yes ! Well, that's good !"

"No, it isn't ! Don't say such a thing—till you know !" she cried, with a certain shrillness which warned him of an unfathomed seriousness in the fact. He sat up as if better to confront the mystery. "I have been at her hotel, and she has been telling me that she's just come from Berlin, and that Mr. Kenby's been there, and— Now I won't have you making a joke of it, or breaking out about it, as if it were not a thing to be looked for ; though of course with the others on our hands you're not to blame for not thinking of it. But you can see yourself that she's young and good-looking. She did speak beautifully of her son, and if it were not for him, I don't believe she would hesitate—"

"For heaven's sake, what *are* you driving at ?" March broke in, and she answered him as vehemently :

320

"He's asked her to marry him!"

"Kenby? Mrs. Adding?"

"Yes!"

"Well, now, Isabel, this won't do! They ought to be ashamed of themselves. With that morbid, delicate boy! It's shocking—"

"Will you listen? Or do you want me to stop?" He arrested himself at her threat, and she resumed, after giving her contempt of his turbulence time to sink in, "She refused him, of course—"

"Oh, all right, then!"

"You take it in such a way that I've a great mind not to tell you anything more about it."

"I know you have," said March, stretching himself out again; "but you'll do it all the same. You'd have been awfully disappointed if I had been calm and collected."

"She refused him," Mrs. March began again, "although she respects him, because she feels that she ought to devote herself to her son. Of course she's very young, yet; she was married when she was only nineteen to a man twice her age, and she's not thirty-five yet. I don't think she *ever* cared much for her husband; and she wants you to find out something about him."

"I never heard of him. I—"

Mrs. March made a "tchck!" that would have recalled the most consequent of men from the most logical and coherent interpretation to the true intent of her words. He perceived his mistake, and said, resolutely : "Well, I won't do it. If she's refused him, that's the end of it ; she needn't know anything about him, and she has no right to."

"Now I think differently," said Mrs. March, with an inductive air. "Of course she has to know about him, *now.*" She stopped, and March turned his head and looked expectantly at her. "He said he would not consider her answer final, but would hope to see her again and— She's afraid he may follow her; he says he's going to write to her ; and— What are you looking at me *so* for ?"

"Is he coming here ?"

"Am I to blame if he is ? Yes—he said he would come."

March burst into a laugh. "Well, *they* haven't been beating about the bush ! When I think how Miss Triscoe has been pursuing Burnamy from the first moment she set eyes on him, with the settled belief that she was running from him, and he imagines that he has been boldly following her without the least hope from her, I can't help admiring the simple directness of these elders."

"And if Kenby wants to talk with you, what will you say ?" she cut in, eagerly.

"I'll say I don't like the subject. What am I in Carlsbad for ? I came for the cure, and I'm spending time and money on it. I might

322

as well go and take my three cups of Felsen-
quelle on a full stomach as listen to Kenby."

"I know it's bad for you, and I wish we had
never seen those people," said Mrs. March.
"I don't believe he'll want to talk with you ;
but if—"

"Is Mrs. Adding in this hotel ? I'm not going to have them round in my bread-trough !"

"She isn't. She's at one of the hotels on the
hill."

"Very well, let her stay there, then. They
can manage their love-affairs in their own way.
The only one I care the least for is that sensitive boy."

"Yes, it *is* forlorn for him. But he likes Mr.
Kenby, and— No, it's horrid, and you can't
make it anything else !"

"Well, I'm not trying to." He turned his
face away. "I must get my nap, now." After
she thought he must have fallen asleep, he
said, "The first thing you know, those old Eltwins will be coming round and telling us that
they're going to get divorced." Then he really
slept.

XXXI

THE mid-day dinner at Pupp's was the time to see the Carlsbad world, and the Marches had the habit of sitting long at table to watch it.

There was one family in whom they fancied a sort of literary quality, as if they had come out of some pleasant German story, but they never knew anything about them. The father by his dress must have been a Protestant clergyman; the mother had been a beauty and was still very handsome; the daughter was good-looking, and of a good-breeding which was both girlish and ladylike. They commended themselves by always taking the table d'hôte dinner, as the Marches did, and eating through from the soup and the rank fresh-water fish to the sweet, upon the same principle: the husband ate all the compote and gave the others his dessert, which was

not good for him. A young girl of a different fascination remained as much a mystery.
She was small and of an extreme tenuity,
which became more bewildering as she advanced through her meal, especially at supper, which she made of a long cucumber
pickle, a Frankfort sausage of twice the
pickle's length, and a towering goblet of
beer; in her lap she held a shivering little
hound; she was in the decorous keeping of
an elderly maid, and had every effect of being a gracious Fräulein. A curious contrast
to her Teutonic voracity was the temperance
of a young Latin swell, imaginably from
Trieste, who sat long over his small coffee
and cigarette, and tranquilly mused upon the
pages of an Italian newspaper. At another
table there was a very noisy lady, short and
fat, in flowing draperies of white, who commanded a sallow family of South-Americans,
and loudly harangued them in South-American Spanish; she flared out, a spot of vivid
light, in a picture which nowhere lacked
strong effects; and in her background lurked a mysterious black face and figure, iron-
ically subservient to the old man, the mild
boy, and the pretty young girl in the middle
distance of the family group.

Amidst the shows of a hardened worldliness
there were touching glimpses of domesticity
and heart: a young bride fed her husband

soup from her own plate with her spoon, unabashed by the publicity; a mother and her two pretty daughters hung about a handsome officer, who must have been newly betrothed to one of the girls; and the whole family showed a helpless fondness for him, which he did not despise though he held it in check; the girls dressed alike, and seemed to have for their whole change of costume a difference from time to time in the color of their sleeves. The Marches believed they had seen the growth of the romance which had eventuated so happily; and they saw other romances which did not in any wise eventuate. Carlsbad was evidently one of the great marriage marts of middle Europe, where mothers brought their daughters to be admired, and everywhere the flower of life was blooming for the hand of love. It blew by on all the promenades in dresses and hats as pretty as they could be bought or imagined; but it was chiefly at Pupp's that it flourished. For the most part it seemed to flourish in vain, and to be destined to be put by for another season to dream, bulblike, of the coming summer in the quiet of Moldavain and Transylvanian homes.

Perhaps it was oftener of fortunate effect than the spectators knew; but for their own pleasure they would not have had their pang for it less; and March objected to having a more explicit demand upon his sympathy.

"We could have managed," he said, at the close of their dinner, as he looked compassionately round upon the parterre of young girls— "we could have managed with Burnamy and Miss Triscoe; but to have Mrs. Adding and Kenby launched upon us is too much. Of course I like Kenby, and if the widow alone were concerned I would give him my blessing: a wife more or a widow less is not going to disturb the equilibrium of the universe; but—" He stopped, and then he went on. "Men and women are well enough. They complement each other very agreeably, and they have very good times together. But why should they get in love? It is sure to make them uncomfortable to themselves and annoying to others." He broke off, and stared about him. "My dear, this is really charming—almost as charming as the Posthof." The crowd spread from the open vestibule of the hotel and the shelter of its branching pavilion roofs until it was dimmed in the obscurity of the low grove across the way in an ultimate depth where the musicians were giving the afternoon concert. Between its two stationary divisions moved a current of promenaders, with some such effect as if the colors of a lovely garden should have liquefied and flowed in mingled rose and lilac, pink and yellow, and white and orange, and all the middle tints of modern millinery. Above on one side were the agreeable bulks of architecture, in the buff and gray of Carlsbad ; and far beyond on the other were the upland slopes, with villas and long curves of country roads, belted in with miles of wall. " It would be about as offensive to have a love-interest that one personally knew about intruded here," he said, " as to have a two-spanner carriage driven through the crowd. It ought to be forbidden by the municipality."

Mrs. March listened with her ears, but not her eyes, and she answered : " See that handsome young Greek priest ! Isn't he an archimandrite ? The *portier* said he was."

" Then let him pass for an archimandrite. —Now," he recurred to his grievance again, dreamily, " I've got to take Papa Triscoe in hand, and poison his mind against Burnamy, and I shall have to instil a few drops of venomous suspicion against Kenby into the heart of poor little Rose Adding. Oh," he broke out, " they will spoil everything. They'll be with us morning, noon, and night," and he went on to work the joke of repining at his lot. The worst thing, he said, would be the lovers' pretence of being interested in something besides themselves, which they were no more capable of than so many lunatics. How could they care for pretty girls playing tennis on an upland level, in the waning afternoon ? Or a cartful of peasant women stopping to cross themselves at a way-side shrine ? Or a whist-

A WAYSIDE SHRINE

ling boy with holes in his trousers pausing from some way-side raspberries to touch his hat and say good-morning? Or those preposterous maidens sprinkling linen on the grass from watering-pots while the skies were full of rain? Or that blacksmith shop where Peter the Great made a horseshoe? Or the monument of the young warrior-poet Koerner, with a gentle-looking girl and her mother reading and knitting on a bench before it? These simple pleasures sufficed them, but what could lovers really care for them? A peasant girl flung down on the grassy roadside, fast asleep, while her yoke-fellow, the gray old dog, lay in his harness near her with one drowsy eye half open for her and the other for the contents of their cart; a boy chasing a red squirrel in the old upper town beyond the Tepl, and enlisting the interest of all the neighbors; the negro door-keeper at the Golden Shield who ought to have spoken our Southern English, but who spoke bad German and was from Cairo; the sweet afternoon stillness in the woods; the good German mothers crocheting at the Post-hof concerts: Burnamy as a young poet might have felt the precious quality of these things, if his senses had not been holden by Miss Triscoe; and she might have felt it if only he had done so. But as it was it would be lost upon their preoccupation; with Mrs. Adding and Kenby it would be hopeless.

A day or two after Mrs. March had met Mrs. Adding, she went with her husband to revere a certain magnificent blackamoor whom he had discovered at the entrance of one of the aristocratic hotels on the Schlossberg, where he performed the function of a kind of caryatid, and looked, in the black of his skin and the white of his flowing costume, like a colossal figure carved in ebony and ivory. They took a roundabout way through a street entirely of villa-pensions; every house in Carlsbad but one is a pension if it is not a hotel; but these were of a sort of sentimental prettiness, with each a little garden before it, and a bower with an iron table in it for breakfasting and supping out-doors; and he said that they would be the very places for bridal couples who wished to spend the honeymoon in getting well of the wedding surfeit. She denounced him for saying such a thing as that, and for his inconsistency in complaining of lovers while he was willing to think of young married people. He contended that there was a great difference in the sort of demand that young married people made upon the interest of witnesses, and that they were at least on their way to sanity; and before they agreed, they had come to the hotel with the blackamoor at the door. While they lingered sharing the splendid creature's hospitable pleasure in the spectacle he formed, they were aware of a carriage with liveried coachman and footman at the steps of the hotel ; the liveries were very quiet and distinguished, and they learned that the equipage was waiting for the Prince of Coburg, or the Princess of Montenegro, or Prince Henry of Prussia ; there were differing opinions among the twenty or thirty bystanders. Mrs. March said she did not care which it was ; and she was patient of the dénouement, which began to postpone itself with delicate delays. After repeated agitations at the door among *portiers*, proprietors, and waiters, whose fluttered spirits imparted their thrill to the spectators, while the coachman and footman remained sculpturesquely impassive in their places, the carriage moved aside and let an energetic American lady and her family drive up to the steps. The hotel people paid her a tempered devotion, but she marred the effect by rushing out and sitting on a balcony to wait for the delaying royalties. There began to be more promises of their early appearance ; a footman got down and placed himself at the carriage door ; the coachman stiffened himself on his box ; then he relaxed ; the footman drooped, and even wandered aside. There came a moment when at some signal the carriage drove quite away from the portal and waited near the gate of the stable-yard ; it drove back, and the spectators redoubled their attention. Nothing happened, and some of them dropped off. At last an indescribable significance expressed itself on the official group at the door ; a man in a high hat and dress-coat hurried out ; a footman hurried to meet him ; they spoke inaudibly together. The footman mounted to his place ; the coachman gathered up his reins and drove rapidly out of the hotel-yard, down the street, round the corner, out of sight. The man in the tall hat and dress-coat went in ; the official group at the threshold dissolved ; the statue in ivory and ebony resumed its place ; evidently the Hoheit of Coberg, or Montenegro, or Prussia, was not going to take the air.

"My dear, this is humiliating."

"Not at all ! I wouldn't have missed it for anything. Think how near we came to seeing them !"

"I shouldn't feel so shabby if we *had* seen them. But to hang round here in this plebeian abeyance, and then to be defeated and defrauded at last ! I wonder how long this sort of thing is going on ?"

"What thing ?"

"This base subjection of the imagination to the Tom Foolery of the Ages."

"I don't know what you mean. I'm sure it's very natural to want to see a Prince."

"Only too natural. It's so deeply founded in nature that after denying royalty by word and deed for a hundred years, we Americans are hungrier for it than anybody else. Perhaps we may come back to it !"

" Nonsense !"

They looked up at the Austrian flag on the tower of the hotel, languidly curling and uncurling in the bland evening air, as it had over a thousand years of stupid and selfish monarchy, while all the generous republics of the Middle Ages had perished, and the commonwealths of later times had passed like fever dreams. That dull inglorious empire had antedated or outlived Venice and Genoa, Florence and Siena, the England of Cromwell, the Holland of the Stadtholders, and the France of many revolutions, and all the fleeting democracies which sprang from these.

March began to ask himself how his curiosity differed from that of the Europeans about him ; then he became aware that these had detached themselves, and left him exposed to the presence of a fellow-countryman. It was Otterson, with Mrs. Otterson ; he turned upon March with hilarious recognition. " Hello ! Most of the Americans in Carlsbad seem to be hanging round here for a sight of these kings. Well, *we* don't have a great many of 'em, and it's natural we shouldn't want to miss any. But now, you Eastern fellows, you go to Europe every summer, and yet you don't seem to get enough of 'em. Think it's human nature, or did it get so ground into us in the old times

335

that we can't get it out, no difference what we say?"

"That's very much what I've been asking myself," said March. "Perhaps it's any kind of show. We'd wait nearly as long for the President to come out, wouldn't we?"

"I reckon we would. But we wouldn't for his nephew, or his second cousin."

"Well, they wouldn't be in the way of the succession."

"I guess your right." The Iowan seemed better satisfied with March's philosophy than March felt himself, and he could not forbear adding:

"But I don't deny that we should wait for the President because he's a kind of king too. I don't know that we shall ever get over wanting to see kings of some kind. Or at least my wife won't. May I present you to Mrs. March?"

"Happy to meet you, Mrs. March," said the Iowan. "Introduce you to Mrs. Otterson. *I'm* the fool in *my* family, and I know just how you feel about a chance like this. I don't mean that you're—"

They all laughed at the hopeless case, and Mrs. March said, with one of her unexpected likings: "I understand, Mr. Otterson. And I would rather be our kind of fool than the kind that pretends not to care for the sight of a king."

"Like you and me, Mrs. Otterson," said March.

"Indeed, indeed," said the lady, " I'd like to see a king too, if it didn't take all night. Good-evening," she said, turning her husband about with her, as if she suspected a purpose of patronage in Mrs. March, and was not going to have it.

Otterson looked over his shoulder to explain, despairingly : "The trouble with me is that when I do get a chance to talk English, there's such a flow of language it carries me away, and I don't know just where I'm landing."

XXXII

THERE were several kings and their kindred at Carlsbad that summer. One
day the Duchess of Orleans drove over
from Marienbad, attended by the Duke on his
bicycle. After luncheon, they reappeared for
a moment before mounting to her carriage
with their secretaries : two young French gentlemen whose dress and bearing better satisfied
Mrs. March's exacting passion for an aristocratic air in their order. The Duke was fat
and fair, as a Bourbon should be, and the
Duchess fatter though not so fair, as became a
Hapsburg, but they were both more plebeian-
looking than their retainers, who were slender
as well as young, and as perfectly appointed
as English tailors could imagine them.

" It wouldn't do for the very highest sort of
Highhotes," March suggested, " to look their
own consequence personally ; they have to

leave that, like everything else, to their inferiors."

By a happy heterophemy of Mrs. March's the German Hoheit had now become Highhote, which was so much more descriptive that they had permanently adopted it, and found comfort to their republican pride in the mockery which it poured upon the feudal structure of society. They applied it with a certain compunction, however, to the King of Servia, who came a few days after the Duke and Duchess : he was such a young king, and of such a little country. They watched for him from the windows of the reading-room, while the crowd outside stood six deep on the three sides of the square before the hotel, and the two plain public carriages which brought the King and his suite drew tamely up at the portal, where the proprietor and some civic dignitaries received him. His moderated approach, so little like that of royalty on the stage, to which Americans are used, allowed Mrs. March to make sure of the pale, slight, insignificant, amiable-looking youth in spectacles as the sovereign she was ambuscading. Then no appeal to her principles could keep her from peeping through the reading-room door into the rotunda, where the King graciously but speedily dismissed the civic gentlemen and the proprietor, and vanished into the elevator. She was destined to see him so often afterwards that she scarcely took the trouble to time her dining and supping by that of the simple potentate, who had his meals in one of the public rooms, with three gentlemen of his suite, in sack-coats like himself, after the informal manner of the place.

Still another potentate, who happened that summer to be sojourning abroad, in the interval of a successful rebellion, was at the opera one night with some of his faithful followers. Burnamy had offered Mrs. March, who supposed that he merely wanted her and her husband with him, places in a box ; but after she eagerly accepted, it seemed that he wished her to advise him whether it would do to ask Miss Triscoe and her father to join them. " Why not ?" she returned, with an arching of the eyebrows.

" Why," he said, " perhaps I had better make a clean breast of it."

" Perhaps you had," she said, and they both laughed, though he laughed with a knot between his eyes.

" The fact is, you know, this isn't my treat, exactly. It's Mr. Stoller's." At the surprise in her face he hurried on. " He's got back his first letter in the paper, and he's so much pleased with the way he reads in print, that he wants to celebrate."

" Yes," said Mrs. March, non-committally.

Burnamy laughed again. " But he's bashful, and he isn't sure that you would all take it in the right way. He wants you as friends of mine ; and he hasn't quite the courage to ask you himself."

This seemed to Mrs. March so far from bad that she said : " That's very nice of him. Then he's satisfied with—with your help ? I'm glad of that."

" Thank you. He's met the Triscoes, and he thought it would be pleasant to you if they went, too."

" Oh, certainly."

" He thought," Burnamy went on, with the air of feeling his way, " that we might all go to the opera, and then—then go for a little supper afterwards at Schwarzkopf's."

He named the only place in Carlsbad where you can sup so late as ten o'clock ; as the opera begins at six, and is over at half past eight, none but the wildest roisterers frequent the place at that hour.

" Oh !" said Mrs. March. " I don't know how a late supper would agree with my husband's cure. I should have to ask him."

" We could make it very hygienic," Burnamy explained.

In repeating his invitation she blamed Burnamy's uncandor so much that March took his part, as perhaps she intended, and said, " Oh, nonsense," and that he should like to go in for the whole thing ; and General Triscoe accepted as promptly for himself and his

341

daughter. That made six people, Burnamy counted up, and he feigned a decent regret that there was not room for Mrs. Adding and her son ; he would have liked to ask them.

Mrs. March did not enjoy it so much as coming with her husband alone, when they took two florin seats in the orchestra for the comedy. The comedy always began half an hour earlier than the opera, and they had a five-o'clock supper at the Theatre-Café before they went, and they got to sleep by nine o'clock ; now they would be up till half past ten at least, and that orgy at Schwarzkopf's might not be at all good for him. But still she liked being there ; and Miss Triscoe made her take the best seat ; Burnamy and Stoller made the older men take the other seats beside the ladies, while they sat behind, or stood up, when they wished to see, as people do in the back of a box. Stoller was not much at ease in evening dress, but he bore himself with a dignity which was not perhaps so gloomy as it looked ; Mrs. March thought him handsome in his way, and required Miss Triscoe to admire him. As for Burnamy's beauty it was not necessary to insist upon that ; he had the distinction of slender youth ; and she liked to think that no Highhote there was of a more patrician presence than this yet unprinted contributor to *Every Other Week*. He and Stoller seemed on perfect terms ; or else in his

342

joy he was able to hide the uneasiness which she had fancied in him from the first time she saw them together, and which had never been quite absent from his manner in Stoller's presence. Her husband always denied that it existed, or if it did that it was anything but Burnamy's effort to get on common ground with an inferior whom fortune had put over him.

The young fellow talked with Stoller, and tried to bring him into the range of the general conversation. He leaned over the ladies, from time to time, and pointed out the notables whom he saw in the house ; she was glad, for his sake, that he did not lean less over her than over Miss Triscoe. He explained certain military figures in the boxes opposite, and certain ladies of rank who did not look their rank ; Miss Triscoe, to Mrs. March's thinking, looked their united ranks, and more ; her dress was very simple, but of a touch which saved it from being insipidly girlish ; her beauty was dazzling.

" Do you see that old fellow in the corner chair just behind the orchestra?" asked Burnamy. "He's ninety - six years old, and he comes to the theatre every night, and falls asleep as soon as the curtain rises, and sleeps through till the end of the act."

" How dear !" said the girl, leaning forward to fix the nonagenarian with her glasses, while many other glasses converged upon her. "Oh, wouldn't you like to know him, Mr. March?"

"I should consider it a liberal education. They have brought these things to a perfect system in Europe. There is nothing to make life pass smoothly like inflexible constancy to an entirely simple custom. My dear," he added to his wife, "I wish we'd seen this sage before. He'd have helped us through a good many hours of unintelligible comedy. I'm always coming as Burnamy's guest, after this."

The young fellow swelled with pleasure in his triumph, and casting an eye about the theatre to cap it, he caught sight of that other potentate. He whispered joyfully, "Ah! We've got two kings here to-night," and he indicated in a box of their tier just across from that where the King of Servia sat, the well-known face of the King of New York.

"He isn't bad-looking," said March, handing his glass to General Triscoe. "I've not seen many kings in exile; a matter of a few Carlist princes and ex-sovereign dukes, and the good Henry V. of France, once, when I was staying a month in Venice; but I don't think they any of them looked the part better. I suppose he has his dream of recurring power like the rest."

"Dream!" said General Triscoe with the glass at his eyes. "He's dead sure of it."

"Oh, you don't *really* mean that!"

"I don't know why I should have changed my mind."

"Then it's as if we were in the presence of Charles II. just before he was called back to England, or Napoleon in the last moments of Elba. It's better than that. The thing is almost unique; it's a new situation in history. Here's a sovereign who has no recognized function, no legal status, no objective existence. He has no sort of public being, except in the affection of his subjects. It took an upheaval little short of an earthquake to unseat him. His rule, as we understand it, was bad for all classes; the poor suffered more than the rich; the people have now had three years of self-government; and yet this wonderful man has such a hold upon the masses that he is going home to win the cause of oppression at the head of the oppressed. When he's in power again, he will be as subjective as ever, with the power of civic life and death, and an idolatrous following perfectly ruthless in the execution of his will."

"We've only begun," said the general. "This kind of king is municipal, now; but he's going to be national. And then, good-bye, Republic!"

"The only thing like it," March resumed, too incredulous of the evil future to deny himself the æsthetic pleasure of the parallel, "is the rise of the Medici in Florence, but even the Medici were not mere manipulators of pulls;

they had some sort of public office, with some sort of legislated tenure of it. The King of New York is sovereign by force of will alone, and he will reign in the voluntary submission of the majority. Is our national dictator to be of the same nature and quality?"

"That would be the scientific evolution, wouldn't it?"

The ladies listened with the perfunctory attention which women pay to any sort of inquiry which is not personal. Stoller had scarcely spoken yet; he now startled them all by demanding, with a sort of vindictive force, "Why shouldn't he have the power, if they're willing to let him?"

"Yes," said General Triscoe, with a tilt of his head towards March. "That's what we must ask ourselves more and more."

March leaned back in his chair, and looked up over his shoulder at Stoller. "Well, I don't know. Do you think it's quite right for a man to use an unjust power, even if others are willing that he should?"

Stoller stopped, with an air of bewilderment as if surprised on the point of affirming that he thought just this. He asked instead, "What's wrong about it?"

"Well, that's one of those things that have to be felt, I suppose. But if a man came to you, and offered to be your slave for a certain consideration — say a comfortable house and a

348

steady job, that wasn't too hard—should you feel it morally right to accept the offer? I don't say *think* it right, for there might be a kind of logic for it."

Stoller seemed about to answer; he hesitated; and before he had made any response, the curtain rose.

XXXIII

THERE are few prettier things than Carlsbad by night from one of the many bridges which span the Tepl in its course through the town. If it is a starry night, the torrent glides swiftly away with an inverted firmament in its bosom, to which the lamps along its shores and in the houses on either side contribute a planetary splendor of their own. By nine o'clock everything is hushed ; not a wheel is heard at that dead hour ; the few feet shuffling stealthily through the Alte Wiese whisper a caution of silence to those issuing with a less guarded tread from the opera ; the little bowers that overhang the stream are as dark and mute as the restaurants across the way which serve meals in them by day ; the whole place is as forsaken as other cities at midnight. People get quickly home to bed, or if they have a mind to snatch a belated joy, they slip into the Theatre-Café, where the sleepy Fräuleins serve them, in an exemplary drowse, with plates of cold ham and bottles of the gently gaseous waters of Giesshübl. Few are of the bold badness which delights in a supper at Schwarzkopf's, and even these are glad of the drawn curtains which hide their orgy from the chance passer.

The invalids of Burnamy's party kept together, strengthening themselves in a mutual purpose not to be tempted to eat anything which was not strictly *kurgemäss.* Mrs. March played upon the interest which each of them felt in his own case so artfully that she kept them talking of their cure, and left Burnamy and Miss Triscoe to a moment on the bridge, by which they profited, while the others strolled on, to lean against the parapet and watch the lights in the skies and the water, and be alone together. The stream shone above and below, and found its way out of and into the darkness under the successive bridges ; the town climbed into the night with lamp-lit windows here and there, till the woods of the hill-sides darkened down to meet it, and fold it in an embrace from which some white edifice showed palely in the farthest gloom.

He tried to make her think they could see that great iron crucifix which watches over it day and night from its piny cliff. He had a fancy for a poem, very impressionistic, which should convey the notion of the crucifix's vigil. He submitted it to her; and they remained talking till the others had got out of sight and hearing; and she was letting him keep the hand on her arm which he had put there to hold her from falling over the parapet, when they were both startled by approaching steps, and a voice calling, "Look here! Who's running this supper party, anyway?"

His wife had detached March from her group for the mission, as soon as she felt that the young people were abusing her kindness. They answered him with hysterical laughter, and Burnamy said, "Why, it's Mr. Stoller's treat, you know."

At the restaurant, where the proprietor obsequiously met the party on the threshold and bowed them into a pretty inner room, with a table set for their supper, Stoller had gained courage to play the host openly. He appointed General Triscoe to the chief seat; he would have put his daughter next to him, if the girl had not insisted upon Mrs. March's having the place, and going herself to sit next to March, whom she said she had not been able to speak a word to the whole evening. But she did not talk a great deal to him; he smiled to find how soon he dropped out of the conversation, and Burnamy, from his greater remoteness across the table, dropped into it. He really preferred the study of Stoller, whose instinct of a greater

ALTE WIESE

worldly quality in the Triscoes interested him ; he could see him listening now to what General Triscoe was saying to Mrs. March, and now to what Burnamy was saying to Miss Triscoe ; his strong, selfish face, as he turned it on the young people, expressed a mingled grudge and greed that was very curious.

Stoller's courage, which had come and gone at moments throughout, rose at the end, and while they lingered at the table well on to the hour of ten, he said, in the sort of helpless offence he had with Burnamy, "What's the reason we can't all go out to-morrow to that old castle you was talking about ?"

"To Engelhaus ? I don't know any reason, as far as I'm concerned," answered Burnamy ; but he refused the initiative offered him, and Stoller was obliged to ask March :

"You heard about it ?"

"Yes." General Triscoe was listening, and March added for him, "It was the hold of an old robber baron ; Gustavus Adolphus knocked it down, and it's very picturesque, I believe."

"It sounds promising," said the general. "Where is it ?"

"Isn't to-morrow your mineral bath ?" Mrs. March interposed between her husband and temptation.

"No ; the day after. Why, it's about ten or

twelve miles out on the old post-road that Napoleon took for Prague."

"Napoleon knew a good road when he saw it," said the general, and he alone of the company lighted a cigar. He was decidedly in favor of the excursion, and he arranged for it with Stoller, whom he had the effect of using for his pleasure as if he were doing him a favor. They were six, and two carriages would take them; a two-spanner for four, and a one-spanner for two; they could start directly after dinner, and get home in time for supper.

Stoller asserted himself to say: "That's all right, then. I want you to be my guests, and I'll see about the carriages." He turned to Burnamy: "Will you order them?"

"Oh," said the young fellow, with a sort of dryness, "the *portier* will get them."

"I don't understand why General Triscoe was so willing to accept. Surely, he can't *like* that man!" said Mrs. March to her husband in their own room.

"Oh, I fancy that wouldn't be essential. The general seems to me capable of letting even an enemy serve his turn. Why didn't you speak, if you didn't want to go?"

"Why didn't you?"

"I wanted to go."

"And I knew it wouldn't do to let Miss Triscoe go alone; I could see that she wished to go."

"Do you think Burnamy did?"

"He seemed rather indifferent. And yet he must have realized that he would be with her the whole afternoon."

XXXIV

IF Burnamy and Miss Triscoe took the lead
in the one-spanner, and the others followed
in the two-spanner, it was not from want
of politeness on the part of the young people
in offering to give up their places to each of
their elders in turn. It would have been grotesque for either March or Stoller to drive with
the girl ; for her father it was apparently no
question, after a glance at the more rigid up-
rightness of the seat in the one-spanner ; and
he accepted the place beside Mrs. March on the
back seat of the two-spanner without demur.
He asked her leave to smoke, and then he
scarcely spoke to her. But he talked to the
two men in front of him almost incessantly,
haranguing them upon the inferiority of our
conditions and the futility of our hopes as a
people, with the effect of bewildering the
cruder arrogance of Stoller, who could have

got on with Triscoe's contempt for the worth-
lessness of our working - classes, but did not
know what to do with his scorn of the vulgarity
and venality of their employers. He accused
some of Stoller's most honored and envied cap-
italists of being the source of our worst corruptions, and guiltier than the voting - cattle
whom they bought and sold.

"I think we can get rid of the whole trouble
if we go at it the right way," Stoller said, di-
verging for the sake of the point he wished to
bring in. "I believe in having the government run on business principles. They've got
it here in Carlsbad, already, just the right sort
of thing, and it works. I been lookin' into it, and
I got this young man, yonder "—he twisted his
hand in the direction of the one-spanner—" to
help me put it in shape. I believe it's going
to make our folks think, the best ones among
them. Here !" He drew a newspaper out of
his pocket, folded to show two columns in their
full length, and handed it to Triscoe, who took
it with no great eagerness, and began to run
his eye over it. "You tell me what you think
of that. I've put it out for a kind of a feeler.
I got some money in that paper, and I just
thought I'd let our people see how a city can
be managed on business principles."

He kept his eye eagerly upon Triscoe, as if
to follow his thought while he read, and keep
him up to the work, and he ignored the Marches

so entirely that they began in self-defence to talk with each other.

Their carriage had climbed from Carlsbad in long irregular curves to the breezy upland where the great highroad to Prague ran through fields of harvest. They had come by heights and slopes of forest, where the serried stems of the tall firs showed brown and whitish-blue and grew straight as stalks of grain; and now on either side the farms opened under a sky of unwonted cloudlessness. Narrow strips of wheat and rye, which the men were cutting with sickles, and the women in red bodices were binding, alternated with ribands of yellowing oats and grass, and breadths of beets and turnips, with now and then lengths of ploughed land. In the meadows the peasants were piling their carts with heavy rowen, the girls lifting the hay on the forks, and the men giving themselves the lighter labor of ordering the load. From the upturned earth, where there ought to have been troops of strutting crows, a few sombre ravens rose. But they could not rob the scene of its gayety; it smiled in the sunshine with colors which vividly followed the slope of the land till they were dimmed in the forests on the far-off mountains. Nearer and farther, the cottages and villages shone in the valleys, or glimmered through the veils of the distant haze. Over all breathed the keen pure air of the hills, with a sentiment of changeless

360

eld, which charmed March back to his boyhood, where he lost the sense of his wife's presence, and answered her vaguely. She talked contentedly on in the monologue to which the wives of absent-minded men learn to resign themselves. They were both roused from their vagary by the voice of General Triscoe. He was handing back the folded newspaper to Stoller, and saying, with a queer look at him over his glasses, "I should like to see what your contemporaries have to say to all that."

"Well, sir," Stoller returned, "maybe I'll have the chance to show you. They got my instructions over there to send everything to me."

Burnamy and Miss Triscoe gave little heed to the landscape as landscape. They agreed that the human interest was the great thing on a landscape, after all; but they ignored the peasants in the fields and meadows, who were no more to them than the driver on the box, or the people in the two-spanner behind. They were talking of the hero and heroine of a novel they had both read, and he was saying, "I suppose you think he was justly punished."

"Punished?" she repeated. "Why, they got married, after all!"

"Yes, but you could see that they were not going to be happy."

"Then it seems to me that she was punished, too."

"Well, yes ; you might say that. The author couldn't help that."

Miss Triscoe was silent a moment before she said : " I always thought the author was rather hard on the hero. The girl was very exacting."

"Why," said Burnamy, "I supposed that women hated anything like deception in men too much to tolerate it at all. Of course, in this case, he didn't deceive her ; he let her deceive herself ; but wasn't that worse ?"

" Yes, that *was* worse. She could have forgiven *him* for deceiving her."

" Oh !"

" He might have *had* to do that. She wouldn't have minded his fibbing outright, so much, for then it wouldn't have seemed to come from his nature. But if he just let her believe what wasn't true, and didn't say a word to prevent her, of course it was worse. It showed something weak, something cowardly in him."

Burnamy gave a little cynical laugh. "I suppose it did. But don't you think it's rather rough, expecting us to have *all* the kinds of courage ?"

"Yes, it is," she assented. "That is why I say she was too exacting. But a man oughtn't to defend him."

Burnamy's laugh had more pleasure in it now. "Another woman might ?"

" No. Excuse him."

He turned to look back at the two-spanner ;

it was rather far behind, and he spoke to their driver, bidding him go slowly till it caught up with them. By the time it did so, they were so close to the ruin that they could distinguish the lines of its wandering and broken walls. Ever since they had climbed from the wooded depths of the hills above Carlsbad to the open plateau, it had shown itself in greater and greater detail. The detached mound of rock on which it stood rose like an island in the midst of the vast plain, and commanded the highways in every direction.

"I believe," Burnamy broke out, with a bitterness apparently relevant to the ruin alone, "that if you hadn't required any quarterings of nobility from him, Stoller would have made a good sort of robber baron. He's a robber baron by nature, now, and he wouldn't have any scruple in levying tribute on us here in our one-spanner, if his castle was in good repair and his crossbowmen were not on a strike. But they *would* be on a strike, probably, and then he would lock them out, and employ none but non-union crossbowmen."

If Miss Triscoe understood that he arraigned the morality as well as the civility of his employer, she did not take him more seriously than he meant, apparently, for she laughed as she said, "I don't see how you can have anything to do with him, if you feel so about him."

"Oh," Burnamy replied, in kind, "he buys my poverty and not my will. And perhaps if I thought better of myself, I should respect him more."

"Have you been doing something very wicked?" she asked.

"What should you have to say to me, if I had?" he bantered.

"Oh, I should have nothing at all to say to you," she mocked back.

They turned a corner of the highway, and drove rattling through a village street up a long slope to the rounded hill which it crowned. A church at its base looked out upon an irregular square.

A gaunt figure of a man, with a staring mask, which seemed to hide a darkling mind within, came out of the church, and locked it behind him. He proved to be the sacristan, and the keeper of all the village's claims upon the visitors' interest; he mastered, after a moment, their wishes in respect to the castle, and showed them the path that led to it; at the top, he said, they would find a custodian of the ruins who would admit them.

XXXV

THE path to the castle slanted upward
across the shoulder of the hill, to a certain point, and there some rude stone
steps mounted more directly. Wilding lilac-
bushes, as if from some forgotten garden, bordered the ascent ; the chickory opened its blue
flower ; the clean bitter odor of vermouth rose
from the trodden turf ; but Nature spreads no
such lavish feast in wood or field in the Old
World as she spoils us with in the New ; a few
kinds, repeated again and again, seem to be all
her store, and man must make the most of
them. Miss Triscoe seemed to find flowers
enough in the simple bouquet which Burnamy
put together for her. She took it, and then
gave it back to him, that she might have both
hands for her skirt, and so did him two favors.

A superannuated forester of the nobleman
who owns the ruin opened a gate for the party

at the top, and levied a tax of thirty kreutzers each upon them, for its maintenance. The castle, by his story, had descended from robber sire to robber son, till Gustavus knocked it to pieces in the sixteenth century; three hundred years later, the present owner restored it; and now its broken walls and arches, built of rubble mixed with brick, and neatly pointed up with cement, form a ruin satisfyingly permanent. The walls were not of great extent, but such as they were they enclosed several dungeons and a chapel, all underground, and a cistern which once enabled the barons and their retainers to water their wine in time of siege.

From that height they could overlook the neighboring highways in every direction, and could bring a merchant train to, with a shaft from a crossbow, or a shot from an arquebuse, at pleasure. With General Triscoe's leave, March praised the strategic strength of the unique position, which he found expressive of the past, and yet suggestive of the present. It was more a difference in method than anything else that distinguished the levy of customs by the authorities then and now. What was the essential difference, between taking tribute of travellers passing on horseback, and collecting dues from travellers arriving by steamer? They did not pay voluntarily in either case; but it might be a proof of progress that they no longer fought the customs officials.

"Then you believe in free trade," said Stoller, severely.

"No. I am just inquiring which is the best way of enforcing the tariff laws."

"I saw in the Paris *Chronicle*, last night," said Miss Triscoe, "that people are kept on the docks now for hours, and ladies cry at the way their things are tumbled over by the inspectors."

"It's shocking," said Mrs. March.

"It seems to be a return to the scenes of feudal times," her husband resumed. "But I'm glad the travellers make no resistance. I'm opposed to private war as much as I am to free trade."

"It all comes round to the same thing at last," said General Triscoe. "Your precious humanity—"

"Oh, I don't claim it exclusively," March protested.

"Well, then, *our* precious humanity is like a man that has lost his road. He thinks he is finding his way out, but he is merely rounding on his course, and coming back to where he started."

Stoller said, "I think we ought to make it so rough for them, over here, that they will come to America and set up, if they can't stand the duties."

"Oh, we ought to make it rough for them anyway," March consented.

If Stoller felt his irony, he did not know what to answer. He followed with his eyes the manœuvre by which Burnamy and Miss Triscoe eliminated themselves from the discussion, and strayed off to another corner of the ruin, where they sat down on the turf in the shadow of the wall; a thin, upland breeze drew across them, but the sun was hot. The land fell away from the height, and then rose again on every side in carpetlike fields and in long curving bands, whose parallel colors passed unblended into the distance. "I don't suppose," Burnamy said, "that life ever does much better than this, do you? I feel like knocking on a piece of wood and saying 'Unberufen.' I might knock on your bouquet; that's wood."

"It would spoil the flowers," she said, looking down at them in her belt. She looked up and their eyes met.

"I wonder," he said, presently, "what makes us always have a feeling of dread when we are happy?"

"Do *you* have that, too?" she asked.

"Yes. Perhaps it's because we know that change must come, and it must be for the worse."

"That must be it. I never thought of it before, though."

"If we had got so far in science that we could predict psychological weather, and could

"HE FOLLOWED WITH HIS EYES THE MANŒUVRE"

know twenty-four hours ahead when a warm wave of bliss or a cold wave of misery was coming, and prepare for smiles and tears beforehand—it may come to that."

"I hope it won't. I'd rather not know when I was to be happy; it would spoil the pleasure; and wouldn't be any compensation when it was the other way."

A shadow fell across them, and Burnamy glanced round to see Stoller looking down at them, with a slant of the face that brought his aquiline profile into relief. "Oh! Have a turf, Mr. Stoller?" he called gayly up to him.

"I guess we've seen about all there is," he answered. "Hadn't we better be going?" He probably did not mean to be mandatory.

"All right," said Burnamy, and he turned to speak to Miss Triscoe again without further notice of him.

They all descended to the church at the foot of the hill where the weird sacristan was waiting to show them the cold, bare interior, and to account for its newness with the fact that the old church had been burnt, and this one built only a few years before. Then he locked the doors after them, and ran forward to open against their coming the chapel of the village cemetery, which they were to visit after they had fortified themselves for it at the village café.

They were served by a little hunchback

maid ; and she told them who lived in the chief house of the village. It was uncommonly pretty, where all the houses were picturesque, and she spoke of it with respect as the dwelling of a rich magistrate who was clearly the great man of the place. March admired the cat which rubbed against her skirt while she stood and talked, and she took his praises modestly for the cat ; but they wrought upon the envy of her brother so that he ran off to the garden, and came back with two fat, sleepy-eyed puppies which he held up, with an arm across each of their stomachs, for the acclaim of the spectators.

"Oh, *give* him something !" Mrs. March entreated. "He's such a dear."

"No, no ! I am not going to have my little hunchback and her cat outdone," he refused ; and then he was about to yield.

"Hold on !" said Stoller, assuming the host. "I got the change."

He gave the boy a few kreutzers, when Mrs. March had meant her husband to reward his *naïveté* with half a florin at least ; but he seemed to feel that he had now ingratiated himself with the ladies, and he put himself in charge of them for the walk to the cemetery chapel ; he made Miss Triscoe let him carry her jacket when she found it warm.

The chapel is dedicated to the Holy Trinity ; and the Jesuit brother who designed it, two or three centuries ago, indulged a devotional fancy in the triangular form of the structure and the decorative details. Everything is three-cornered; the whole chapel, to begin with, and then the ark of the high altar in the middle of it, and each of the three side-altars. The clumsy baroque taste of the architecture is a German version of the impulse that was making Italy fantastic at the time; the carving is coarse, and the color harsh, and unsoftened by years, though it is blurred and obliterated in places.

The sacristan said that the chapel was never used for anything but funeral services, and he led the way out into the cemetery, where he wished to display the sepultural devices. The graves here were planted with flowers, and some were in a mourning of black pansies; but a space fenced apart from the rest held a few neglected mounds, overgrown with weeds and brambles. This space, he said, was for suicides; but to March it was not so ghastly as the dapper grief of certain tombs in consecrated ground where the stones had photographs of the dead on porcelain let into them. One was the picture of a beautiful young woman, who had been the wife of the local magnate; an eternal love was vowed to her in the inscription, but now, the sacristan said, with nothing of irony, the magnate was married again, and lived in that prettiest house in the village. He seemed proud

of the monument, as the thing worthiest the attention of the strangers, and he led them with
less apparent hopefulness to the unfinished
chapel representing a Gethsemane, with the
figure of Christ praying and his apostles sleeping. It is a subject much celebrated in terra-
cotta about Carlsbad, and it was not a novelty
to his party; still, from its surroundings, it had
a fresh pathos, and March tried to make him
understand that they appreciated it. He knew
that his wife wished the poor man to think he
had done them a great favor in showing it; he
had been touched with all the vain shows of
grief in the poor, ugly little place ; most of all
he had felt the exile of those who had taken
their own lives and were parted in death from
the more patient sufferers who had waited for
God to take them. With a curious, unpainful
self-analysis he noted that the older members
of the party, who in the course of nature were
so much nearer death, did not shrink from its
shows; but the young girl and the young man
had not borne to look on them, and had quickly escaped from the place, somewhere outside
the gate. Was it the beginning, the promise,
of that reconciliation with death which nature
brings to life at last, or was it merely the effect,
or defect, of ossified sensibilities, of toughened
nerves ?

"That is all ?" he asked of the spectral sacristan.

"That is all," the man said, and March felt in his pocket for a coin commensurate to the service he had done them; it ought to be something handsome.

"No, no," said Stoller, detecting his gesture. "Your money a'n't good."

He put twenty or thirty kreutzers into the hand of the man, who regarded them with a disappointment none the less cruel because it was so patient. In France, he would have been insolent; in Italy, he would have frankly said it was too little; here, he merely looked at the money and whispered a sad "Danke."

Burnamy and Miss Triscoe rose from the grassy bank outside where they were sitting, and waited for the elders to get into their two-spanner.

"Oh, have I lost my glove in there?" said Mrs. March, looking at her hands and such parts of her dress as a glove might cling to.

"Let me go and find it for you," Burnamy entreated.

"Well," she consented, and she added, "If the sacristan has found it, give him something for me—something really handsome, poor fellow."

As Burnamy passed her, she let him see that she had both her gloves, and her heart yearned upon him for his instant smile of intelligence: some men would have blundered out that she had the lost glove in her hand. He came back directly, saying, "No, I didn't find it."

375

She laughed, and held both gloves up. " No wonder ! I had it all the time. Thank you ever so much."

"How are we going to ride back?" asked Stoller.

Burnamy almost turned pale ; Miss Triscoe smiled impenetrably. No one else spoke, and Mrs. March said, with placid authority, "Oh, I think the way we came is best."

"Did that absurd creature," she apostrophized her husband as soon as she got him alone after their arrival at Pupp's, "think I was going to let him drive back with Agatha?"

" I wonder," said March, "if that's what Burnamy calls her now ?"

" I shall despise him if it isn't."

XXXVI

BURNAMY took up his mail to Stoller after the supper which they had eaten in a silence natural with two men who have been off on a picnic together. He did not rise from his writing-desk when Burnamy came in, and the young man did not sit down after putting his letters before him. He said, with an effort of forcing himself to speak at once, "I have looked through the papers, and there is something that I think you ought to see."

"What do you mean?" said Stoller.

Burnamy laid down three or four papers opened to pages where certain articles were strongly circumscribed in ink. The papers varied, but their editorials did not, in purport at least. Some were grave and some were gay; one indignantly denounced; another affected an ironical bewilderment; the third

377

simply had fun with the Hon. Jacob Stoller. They all, however, treated his letter on the city government of Carlsbad as the praise of municipal socialism, and the paper which had fun with him gleefully congratulated the dangerous classes on the accession of the Honorable Jacob to their ranks.

Stoller read the articles, one after another, with parted lips and gathering drops of perspiration on his upper lip, while Burnamy waited on foot. He flung the papers all down at last. "Why, they're a pack of fools! They don't know what they're talking about! I want city government carried on on business principles, by the people, for the people. *I* don't care what they say! I know I'm right, and I'm going ahead on this line if it takes all—" The note of defiance died out of his voice at the sight of Burnamy's pale face. "What's the matter with you?"

"There's nothing the matter with me."

"Do you mean to tell me it *is* "—he could not bring himself to use the word—"what they say?"

"I suppose," said Burnamy, with a dry mouth, "it's what you may call municipal socialism."

Stoller jumped from his seat. "And you knew it when you let me do it?"

"I supposed you knew what you were about."

"It's a lie!" Stoller advanced upon him, wildly, and Burnamy took a step backward.

378

"Look out!" shouted Burnamy. "You never asked me anything about it. You told me what you wanted done, and I did it. How could I believe you were such an ignoramus as not to know the a b c of the thing you were talking about?" He added, in cynical contempt : "But you needn't worry. You can make it right with the managers by spending a little more money than you expected to spend."

Stoller started as if the word money reminded him of something. "I can take care of myself, young man. How much do I owe you?"

"Nothing!" said Burnamy, with an effort for grandeur which failed him.

The next morning as the Marches sat over their coffee at the Posthof, he came dragging himself toward them with such a haggard air that Mrs. March called, before he reached their table, "Why, Mr. Burnamy, what's the matter?"

He smiled miserably. "Oh, I haven't slept very well. May I have my coffee with you? I want to tell you something ; I want you to make me. But I can't speak till the coffee comes. Fräulein !" he besought a waitress going off with a tray near them. "Tell Lili, please, to bring me some coffee—only coffee."

He tried to make some talk about the weather, which was rainy, and the Marches helped him, but the poor endeavor lagged wretchedly in the interval between the ordering and the coming of the coffee. "Ah, thank you, Lili," he said, with a humility which confirmed Mrs. March in her instant belief that he had been offering himself to Miss Triscoe and been rejected. After gulping his coffee, he turned to her: "I want to say good-bye. I'm going away."

"From Carlsbad?" asked Mrs. March with a keen distress.

The water came into his eyes. "Don't, *don't* be good to me, Mrs. March! I can't stand it. But you won't, when you know."

He began to speak of Stoller, first to her, but addressing himself more and more to the intelligence of March, who let him go on without question, and laid a restraining hand upon his wife when he saw her about to prompt him. At the end, "That's all," he said, huskily, and then he seemed to be waiting for March's comment. He made none, and the young fellow was forced to ask, "Well, what do you think, Mr. March?"

"What do you think yourself?"

"I think I behaved badly," said Burnamy, and a movement of protest from Mrs. March nerved him to add: "I could make out that it was not my business to tell him what he was doing; but I guess it was; I guess I ought to have stopped him, or given him a chance to

382

stop himself. I suppose I might have done it, if he had treated me decently when I turned up a day late, here; or hadn't acted towards me as if I were a hand in his buggy-works that had come in an hour after the whistle had sounded."

He set his teeth, and an indignant sympathy shone in Mrs. March's eyes; but her husband only looked the more serious.

He asked gently, "Do you offer that fact as an explanation, or as a justification?"

Burnamy laughed forlornly. "It certainly wouldn't justify me. You might say that it made the case all the worse for me." March forbore to say, and Burnamy went on. "But I didn't suppose they would be onto him so quick, or perhaps at all. I thought — if I thought anything—that it would amuse some of the fellows in the office, who know about those things." He paused, and in March's continued silence he went on. "The chance was one in a hundred that anybody else would know where he had brought up."

"But you let him take that chance," March suggested.

"Yes, I let him take it. Oh, you know how mixed all these things are!"

"Yes."

"Of course I didn't think it out at the time. But I don't deny that I had a satisfaction in the notion of the hornets' nest he was poking his thick head into. It makes me sick, now, to think I had. I oughtn't to have let him; he was perfectly innocent in it. After the letter went, I wanted to tell him, but I couldn't; and then I took the chances too. I don't believe he could have ever got forward in politics; he's too honest—or he isn't dishonest in the right way. But that doesn't let *me* out. I don't defend myself! I did wrong; I behaved badly. But I've suffered for it. I've had a foreboding all the time that it would come to the worst; and I've felt like a murderer with his victim when I've been alone with Stoller. When I could get away from him I could shake it off, and even believe that it hadn't happened. You can't think what a nightmare it's been! Well, I've ruined Stoller politically, but I've ruined myself, too. I've spoiled my own life; I've done what I can never explain to—to the people I want to have believe in me; I've got to steal away like the thief I am. Good-bye!" He jumped to his feet, and put out his hand to March, and then to Mrs. March.

"Why, you're not going away *now!*" she cried, in a daze.

"Yes, I am. I shall leave Carlsbad on the eleven-o'clock train. I don't think I shall see you again." He clung to her hand. "If you see—General Triscoe—I wish you'd tell them I couldn't — that I had to — that I was called away suddenly— Good-bye!" He pressed her

384

hand and dropped it, and mixed with the crowd. Then he came suddenly back, with a final appeal to March : " Should you—do you think I ought to see Stoller, and—and tell him I don't think I used him fairly ?"

"You ought to know—" March began.

But before he could say more, Burnamy said, " You're right," and was off again.

" Oh, how hard you were with him, my dear !" Mrs. March lamented.

" I wish," he said, " if our boy ever went wrong that some one would be as true to him as I was to that poor fellow. He condemned himself ; and he was right ; he has behaved very badly."

" You always overdo things so, when you act righteously !"

" Now, Isabel !"

" Oh yes, I know what you will say. But *I* should have tempered justice with mercy."

Her nerves tingled with pity for Burnamy, but in her heart she was glad that her husband had had strength to side with him against himself, and she was proud of the forbearance with which he had done it. In their earlier married life she would have confidently taken the initiative on all moral questions. She still believed that she was better fitted for their decision by her Puritan tradition and her New England birth, but once in a great crisis when it seemed a question of their living, she had weakened before it, and he, with no such advantages, had somehow met the issue with courage and conscience. She could not believe that he did so by inspiration, but she had since let him take the brunt of all such issues and the responsibility. He made no reply, and she said : "I suppose you'll admit now that there was always something peculiar in the poor boy's manner toward Stoller."

He would confess no more than that there ought to have been. " I don't see how he could stagger through with that load on his conscience. I'm not sure I like his being able to do it."

She was silent in the misgiving which she shared with him, but she said : " I wonder how far it has gone with him and Miss Triscoe ?"

" Well, from his wanting you to give his message to the general in the plural—"

" Don't laugh ! It's wicked to laugh ! It's heartless !" she cried, hysterically. " What will he do, poor fellow ?"

" I've an idea that he will light on his feet, somehow. But, at any rate, he's doing the right thing in going to own up to Stoller."

" Oh, Stoller ! I care nothing for Stoller ! Don't speak to me of Stoller !"

Burnamy found the Bird of Prey, as he no longer had the heart to call him, walking up and down in his room like an eagle caught in a trap. He erected his crest with sufficient fierceness, though, when the young fellow came in at his loudly shouted, " *Herein !*"

" What do you want ?" he demanded, brutally.

This simplified Burnamy's task, while it made it more loathsome. He answered not much less brutally, " I want to tell you that I think I used you badly, that I let you betray yourself, that I feel myself to blame." He could have added, " Curse you !" without change of tone.

Stoller sneered in a derision that showed his lower teeth like a dog's when he snarls. " You want to get back !"

" No," said Burnamy, mildly, and with increasing sadness as he spoke. " I don't want to get back. Nothing would induce me. I'm going away on the first train."

" Well, you're *not !*" shouted Stoller. " You've lied me into this—"

" Look out !" Burnamy turned white.

" *Didn't* you lie me into it, if you let me fool myself, as you say ?" Stoller pursued, and Burnamy felt himself weaken through his wrath. " Well, then, you got to lie me out of it. I been going over the damn thing, all night— and you can do it for me. I *know* you can do it," he broke down, in a plea that was almost a whimper. " Look here ! You see if you can't. I'll make it all right with you. I'll pay you whatever you think is right — whatever you say."

"Oh !" said Burnamy, in otherwise unutterable disgust.

"You *kin*," Stoller went on, breaking down more and more into his adopted Hoosier, in the stress of his anxiety. "I know you kin, Mr. Burnamy." He pushed the paper containing his letter into Burnamy's hands, and pointed out a succession of marked passages. "There ! And here ! And this place ! Don't you see how you could make out that it meant something else, or was just ironical?" He went on to prove how the text might be given the complexion he wished, and Burnamy saw that he had really thought it not impossibly out : "I can't put it in writing as well as you ; but I've done all the work, and all you've got to do is to give it some of them turns of yours. I'll cable the fellows in our office to say I've been misrepresented, and that my correction is coming. We'll get it into shape here together, and then I'll cable that. I don't care for the money. And I'll get our counting-room to see *this* scoundrel "—he picked up the paper that had had fun with him—"and fix him all right, so that he'll ask for a suspension of public opinion, and— You see, don't you?"

The thing did appeal to Burnamy. If it could be done, it would enable him to make Stoller the reparation he longed to make him more than anything else in the world. But he heard himself saying, very gently, almost tenderly, "It might be done, Mr. Stoller. But *I* couldn't do it. It wouldn't be honest — for me."

"Yah !" yelled Stoller, and he crushed the paper into a wad and flung it into Burnamy's face. "*Honest*, you damn humbug ! You let me in for this, when you knew I didn't mean it, and now you won't help me out because it a'n't *honest !* Get out of my room, and get out quick before I—"

He hurled himself towards Burnamy, who straightened himself, with "If you dare !" He knew that he was right in refusing ; but he knew that Stoller was right, too, and that he had not meant the logic of what he had said in his letter, and of what Burnamy had let him imply. He braved Stoller's onset, and he left his presence untouched, but feeling as little like a moral hero as he well could.

XXXVII

GENERAL TRISCOE woke in the bad
humor of an elderly man after a day's
pleasure, and in the self-reproach of a
pessimist who has lost his point of view for a
time, and has to work back to it. He began at
the belated breakfast with his daughter when
she said, after kissing him gayly, in the small
two-seated bower where they breakfasted at
their hotel when they did not go to the Posthof,
" *Didn't* you have a nice time, yesterday, papa?"

She sank into the chair opposite, and beamed
at him across the little iron table, as she lifted
the pot to pour out his coffee.

"What do you call a nice time?" he temporized, not quite able to resist her gayety.

"Well, the kind of time *I* had."

"Did you get rheumatism from sitting on
the grass? I took cold in that old church,
and the tea at that restaurant must have been

"'DIDN'T YOU HAVE A NICE TIME YESTERDAY, PAPA?'"

brewed in a brass kettle. I suffered all night from it. And that ass from Illinois—"

"Oh, *poor* papa! I *couldn't* go with Mr. Stoller alone, but I might have gone in the two - spanner with him and let you have Mr. or Mrs. March in the one-spanner. They're so nice!"

"I don't know. Their interest in each other isn't so interesting to other people as they seem to think."

"Do you feel that way really, papa? Don't you like their being so much in love still?"

"At their time of life? Thank you; it's bad enough in young people."

The girl did not answer; she appeared altogether occupied in pouring out her father's coffee.

He tasted it, and then he drank pretty well all of it; but he said, as he put his cup down, "*I* don't know what they make this stuff of. I wish I had a cup of good, honest American coffee."

"Oh, there's nothing like American food!" said his daughter, with so much conciliation that he looked up sharply.

But whatever he might have been going to say was at least postponed by the approach of a serving - maid, who brought a note to his daughter. She blushed a little at sight of it, and then tore it open and read: "I am going away from Carlsbad, for a fault of my own which forbids me to look you in the face. If you wish to know the worst of me, ask Mrs. March. I have no heart to tell you."

Agatha read these mystifying words of Burnamy's several times over in a silent absorption with them which left her father to look after himself, and he had poured out a second cup of coffee with his own hand, and was reaching for the bread beside her before she came slowly back to a sense of his presence. "Oh, excuse me, papa," she said, and she gave him the butter. "Here's a very strange letter from Mr. Burnamy, which I think you'd better see." She held the note across the table to him, and watched his face as he read it.

After he had read it twice, he turned the sheet over, as people do with letters that puzzle them, in the vain hope of something explanatory on the back. Then he looked up and asked: "What do you suppose he's been doing?"

"I don't believe he's been doing anything. It's something that Mr. Stoller's been doing to him."

"I shouldn't infer that from his own words. What makes you think the trouble is with Stoller?"

"He said — he said yesterday — something about being glad to be through with him, because he disliked him so much he was always afraid of wronging him. And that proves that

394

now Mr. Stoller has made him believe that he's done wrong, and has worked upon him till he *does* believe it."

"It proves nothing of the kind," said the general, recurring to the note. After reading it again, he looked keenly at her : "Am I to understand that you have given him the right to suppose you would want to know the worst —or the best of him?"

The girl's eyes fell, and she pushed her knife against her plate. She began : " No—"

"Then confound his impudence !" the general broke out. "What business has he to write to you at all about this?"

"Because he couldn't go away without it !" she retorted ; and she met her father's eye courageously. "He had a right to think we were his friends ; and if he has done wrong, or is in disgrace any way, isn't it manly of him to wish to tell us first himself?"

Her father could not say that it was not. But he could and did say, very sceptically : "Stuff ! Now, see here, Agatha : what are you going to do ?"

"I'm going to see Mrs. March, and then—"

"You mustn't do anything of the kind, my dear," said her father, gently. "You've no right to give yourself away to that romantic old goose." He put up his hand to interrupt her protest. "This thing has got to be gone to the bottom of. But you're not to do it. I

will see March myself. We must consider
your dignity in this matter—and mine. And
you may as well understand that I'm not going to have any nonsense. It's got to be managed so that it can't be supposed we're anxious
about it, one way or the other, or that he was
authorized to write to you in this way—"

"No, no! He oughn't to have done so. He
was to blame— He couldn't have written to
you, though, papa!"

"Well, I don't know why. But that's no
reason why we should let it be understood
that he has written to you. I will see March;
and I will manage to see his wife, too. I shall
probably find them in the reading-room at
Pupp's, and—"

The Marches were in fact just coming in
from their breakfast at the Posthof, and he
met them at the door of Pupp's, where they
all sat down on one of the iron settees of the
piazza, and began to ask one another questions
of their minds about the pleasures of the day
before, and to beat about the bush where Burnamy lurked in their common consciousness.

Mrs. March was not able to keep long from
starting him. "You knew," she said, "that Mr.
Burnamy had left us?"

"Left! Why?" asked the general.

She was a woman of resource, but in a case
like this she found it best to trust her husband's poverty of invention. She looked at

STEPHANIE WARTE

him, and he answered for her with a promptness that made her quake at first, but finally seemed the only thing, if not the best thing: "He's had some trouble with Stoller." He went on to tell the general just what the trouble was.

At the end the general grunted as from an uncertain mind. "You think he's behaved badly."

"I think he's behaved foolishly—youthfully. But I can understand how strongly he was tempted. He could say that he was not authorized to stop Stoller in his mad career."

At this Mrs. March put her hand through her husband's arm.

"I'm not so sure about that," said the general.

March added: "Since I saw him this morning, I've heard something that disposes me to look at his performance in a friendlier light. It is something that Stoller told me himself, to heighten my sense of Burnamy's wickedness. He seems to have felt that I ought to know what a serpent I was cherishing in my bosom," and he gave Triscoe the facts of Burnamy's injurious refusal to help Stoller put a false complexion on the opinions he had allowed him ignorantly to express.

The general grunted again. "Of course he had to refuse, and he has behaved like a gentleman so far. But that doesn't justify him in having let Stoller get himself into the scrape."

"No," said March. "It's a tough nut for the casuist to try his tooth on. And I must say I feel sorry for Stoller."

Mrs. March plucked her hand from his arm. "I don't, one bit. He was thoroughly selfish from first to last. He has got just what he deserved."

"Ah, very likely," said her husband. "The question is about Burnamy's part in giving him his deserts ; he *had* to leave him to them, of course."

The general fixed her with the impenetrable glitter of his eye-glasses, and left the subject as of no concern to him. "I believe," he said, rising, "I'll have a look at some of your papers," and he went into the reading-room.

"Now," said Mrs. March, "he will go home and poison that poor girl's mind. And you will have yourself to thank for prejudicing him against Burnamy."

"Then why didn't you do it yourself, my dear ?" he teased ; but he was really too sorry for the whole affair, which he nevertheless enjoyed as an ethical problem.

The general looked so little at the papers that before March went off for his morning walk he saw him come out of the reading-room and take his way down the Alte Wiese. He went directly back to his daughter, and re-

ported Burnamy's behavior with entire exact-
ness. He dwelt upon his making the best of
a bad business in refusing to help Stoller out
of it, dishonorably and mendaciously ; but he
did not conceal that it was a bad business.

" Now, you know all about it," he said at the
end, "and I leave the whole thing to you. If
you prefer, you can see Mrs. March. I don't
know but I'd rather you'd satisfy yourself—"

" I will *not* see Mrs. March. Do you think I
would go back of you in that way ? I am satisfied now."

END OF VOL. I.